I0613146

Thomas Adolphus Trollope

The Dream Numbers

Vol. III

Thomas Adolphus Trollope

The Dream Numbers
Vol. III

ISBN/EAN: 9783337045210

Printed in Europe, USA, Canada, Australia, Japan

Cover: Foto ©Andreas Hilbeck / pixelio.de

More available books at **www.hansebooks.com**

THE

DREAM NUMBERS.

A Novel.

BY

T. ADOLPHUS TROLLOPE,

AUTHOR OF "LA BEATA," ETC.

IN THREE VOLUMES.

VOL. III.

LONDON:

CHAPMAN & HALL, 193, PICCADILLY.

1868.

LONDON:
BRADBURY, EVANS, AND CO., PRINTERS, WHITEFRIARS.

CONTENTS.

BOOK THE FIFTH.

CAUGHT IN HIS OWN TRAP.

THE DREAM NUMBERS.

(CONTINUATION OF BOOK IV.)

CHAPTER III.

MEO MAKES A MISTAKE.

MEANWHILE Meo Morini had hastened into
Lucca at a quicker pace than he had ever probably walked before. He was not only exceedingly anxious to consult his father on the point
of law, or rather of police practice, as matters
then went in Italy, but looked forward also
with infinite gusto to the treat of telling Farmer
Bartoli and Simonetti the tidings of Caroli's
detected roguery. Above all, the prospect of
communicating the news to Regina was de-
lightful to him. He would not have lost the
chance of being himself the bearer of it for any
consideration. And he debated within himself

whether it would not be best to tell her first.
For he much feared that her father, if he were
the first to hear it, might go off to Regina in
some retreat, which he, Meo, could not reach—
her chamber, perhaps, for Regina had greatly
affected sitting in that sacred retirement since
she had been an inmate of Signore Morini's
house—and thus forestall him.

He spent almost as much thought while
walking to the city, in endeavouring to picture
to himself how Regina would receive this news,
as Carlo in his room at Sponda Lunga was giving
to the same subject. How would the proud
beauty take it? And how should he tell it? For
that also was a matter for deep consideration.

He had not sense and tact enough to comprehend that if anything could make Regina
hate him more than she did already, it would
be to make himself the volunteer bearer of such
tidings ; but still he felt that he must not make
his great delight in the facts he had to tell too
conspicuous. He must at least assume the
commonplace affectation of Christian charity,
which professes to find a cause of sorrow in the

wickedness and downfall of a fellow creature
and a neighbour. Yes, that of course! He
thought that would be easy to do; miscalcu-
lating, as so many people do, the difficulty of
such histrionic effort. For two speakers on
such a subject to preserve a tone of conventional
decency, when both are animated by the same
inward spirit of hatred, malice, and all uncha-
ritableness, is indeed easy. But Meo's task, as
will be understood, was a very different one.
At the bottom of his heart he knew that Regina
loved this Carlo Caroli,—this detected thief;
—knew at all events that she liked him much
better than she did him, Meo Morini. And
hence came the exquisite pleasure of telling her
that his rival was a thief,—ay, a thief found
out!

How was he to conceal the intense gratified
spite that exuded from every pore of him? How
inflict upon Regina the due amount of suffering
and punishment for having preferred this un-
worthy upstart to him, without too flagrantly
betraying it? He was conscious that the task
before him needed careful and delicate handling;

but like an athlete confident in his powers, he went forward to it with a pleasure that made every yard of the distance he had to traverse seem ten!

And how would she take it? Would she openly profess to grieve? Would she, perhaps, shed tears? Would she dare, in his presence, thus to confess how much she cared for this vagabond? He hardly knew whether there would be most pain or pleasure in seeing her thus driven to betray herself. It made his blood boil to think of her thus shamelessly, as he said to himself, manifesting her regard for his rival. And yet there was a keen pleasure in the contemplation of the picture of her tear-shedding for such a cause. What a humiliation for the haughty Regina! He called her pictured weeping shameless, in his thoughts, one minute, and in the next gloated over the humiliation it would cause her. She who had never vouchsafed to be moved to the smallest emotion or interest of any kind by aught that he could say to her! He could interest her now! Oh, yes! now she would hang upon his words! She would beg him, probably, to tell her all the circumstances. And then he would wring her heart by pointing out, in the most superiorly indifferent manner, and yet with un- mistakeable clearness, the absolute conclusive- ness of the evidence against her favourite.

But would she dare to weep over the de- tection of this scamp's scoundrelism in his presence!—in his very presence? Meo hoped she would; yes, he could not help making up his mind that he hoped she would. He gloated over the spectacle in his mind's eye. He saw her beautiful proud cold face forced by him into the betrayal of emotion. She would strive hard to restrain her tears. Then he would give another turn to the moral screw which was causing her anguish, and she would break down, and weep before him. There would be talk between them,—question and answer. It would be his to speak,—his to keep her in an agony of suspense. She would at least feel that he had power in his hands, the cold, haughty girl! He would be in the position of her confidant! She could not for very decency cry over Carlo

Caroli's disgrace openly before all the world! She would have to trust to his forbearance and generosity not to speak to others of the emotion into which she had been betrayed.

And then a new thought struck him.

Suppose .... suppose that a more important advantage than the mere gratification of a passing hour could be got out of this fortunate discovery ? Might it not be possible for him to turn the conjunction of circumstances to his own advantage ? How, if he should try to strike in his own favour when the iron of her emotions was hot? Might he not come to terms with her ? Might he not bargain (with adroitly decorous phrase) to sell her that, which she would doubtless be very anxious to obtain, at a price which it would very well suit his book to accept ? After having enjoyed to his heart's content the scene which he had been picturing to himself, might he not associate himself with her in her grief and distress, and undertake that nothing further should be heard of this robbery, if she would accept him, Meo, as her affianced husband ? She would feel, of course,

that henceforward at all events there could be
no prospect or possibility of anything further
between her and Carlo, as matters stood. She
could not contemplate marrying a convicted
thief! But she might save him at the expense
of giving him up! That she should cease to
feel such a regard for a thief, even though he
were not a convicted one, as would drive her to
purchase his immunity from detection at the
cost of giving her hand to one man, while she
still loved another,—this did not suggest itself
to Meo Morini as at all an insuperable objection
to his plan. Such delicacies of sentiment were
altogether out of his sphere of thought and
feeling. And as for his own share in the arrangement he was imagining,—the obtaining of
a wife, who was admitted by the terms of the
bargain to have given her heart to another man,
—any consideration of this kind gave our friend
Meo very little trouble. In the first place, let
it be how it would, if Regina was his wife,
Caroli would not share in Farmer Bartoli's
dollars at all events. And as for Regina's
affections . . . . "bah! let me once make her

my wife,—and I think I shall know how to take care of myself!" said Meo to himself, with a smile which was not pleasant to see.

As for its being in his power, as matters stood at present, to quash all further mention of the robbery, he had no doubt at all. He felt quite sure, from what the widow had said, that she would easily agree to settle the matter between herself and her manager, and say nothing about it to anybody. And as for Bratti, he had already expressed his opinion that Carlo was not a thief ; and would of course readily acquiesce in any intimation either from him or from the widow, that it was all right.

But for the successful working of this well-imagined scheme, it was absolutely necessary that Meo should see Regina before speaking with any of the others to whom he had been thinking of carrying his news. He thought that he probably might trust his father ; but he was not sure ; and besides, he would fain avoid having to confess failure to his father, in case . . . . if, *par impossible*, his diplomacy should not be successful.

He reached Lucca, therefore, determined to speak to no one of his great news, till he had seen Regina. His heart beat with an agitation very unusual with him, as he found himself at his father's door. He could not help feeling very considerably afraid of the coming interview;—to his own puzzled surprise. What upon earth had *he* to be afraid of? Surely he had the whip hand, and of all the parties concerned had the least reason to fear aught that might arise out of the facts. But he *was* afraid of his interview with Regina, though he gloated in thought over the prospect of it.

Chance was as favourable to his plans as he could have desired. It had not escaped him, among his other calculations, that the difficulty of obtaining a *téte-à-téte* interview might be one obstacle in his way, difficult to be overcome. He knew well enough that Regina would avoid any such, if it were possible to her to do so. But chance made it easy, and delivered her into his hands.

His father and Farmer Bartoli, the servant told him, were out together. The Signorina

Regina was sitting in the *salottino* upstairs along with the Signora Morini. Meo thought at first of sending up a message to Regina in his father's name, begging her to come down into the studio. But he feared that she would run away upstairs again the instant she perceived that it was he, and not his father, who awaited her in the studio. So he decided on writing a little note to his mother, which he sent by the servant.

"Dear mother," he said, "when I come up to the *salottino*, presently, I want you to go away, and leave me with Regina for half-an-hour or so ; I mean to try my fortune with her to-day. Your own son, MEO."

In about five minutes he walked up-stairs, and his mother obediently left the room almost immediately afterwards. Regina, as soon as she perceived her purpose, rose to follow her ; but Meo had provided against this by placing himself between her and the door of the *salottino*.

"Signorina Regina," he said promptly in a grave voice, from which all the affectation of gallantry usual to him, when addressing her, was banished, " I beg that you will allow me to speak to you for a few minutes, for I have something of importance to tell you ; which, if I am not mistaken, will interest you, and which I wish to tell you before mentioning it to any one else."

Regina was arrested by his grave, business-like, and unusual manner ; and reseating herself, looked up at him with surprise, awaiting what he had to say.

"Signorina," he began, biting his nails, and looking with sharp gaze into her face, " a discovery has been made to-day .... that is, to say the truth, I have to-day discovered what must be a matter of great sorrow to us all, and specially, I fear .... that is, I hope .... yes! specially a cause of sorrow to you."

" Indeed, signore ; " said Regina, with an unconcealed indifference of tone and manner, that nettled Meo into greater brusqueness in the manner of his communication than he had intended.

" Yes ! a very important matter, by Jove,

and not one to be spoken of in that tone, as you will see when I have told you, Signorina Regina."

"Well, signore, what is it?—nothing about my father?" she added, in a tone of more interest, as the thought that she had not seen her father all the day, crossed her mind.

"No, signorina! it is nothing about your father. Signor Giovanni is right enough, I am happy to say, and likely to remain so. *He* is all right, he is. But there's others that you care about, I take it, signorina, besides your father. Ain't I right?"

"When you think fit to tell me what you wish to say, signore, I shall know whether I care about it or not," said Regina, with an air of resignation to the bore she was enduring in her tone, and in her *pose* as she sate.

"I was with Signor Carlo Caroli this morning!" said Meo, dropping out the words one by one, and fixing his malevolent eyes intently on her face, as he spoke. There was a little,—a very little start, and a little increase of colour in the marble-pale cheeks. Meo marked that much with his greedy eyes.

"I *thought* that you would like to hear the latest news of him ;" he said, with an insolent sneer in his voice, which it was beyond his power to abstain from, though he had strictly schooled himself to be guilty of nothing of the sort.

"Certainly I should be glad to hear that Signor Carlo is well, and none the worse for what he went through in saving my life ;—very glad!" said Regina, not without some feeling of satisfaction, it must be confessed, in the consciousness that she was paying back again by her words some of the annoyance she was suffering.

"Yes, signorina, he is well enough, for the matter of that. If nothing worse happens to him than what he went through, as you say, the night of the flood, he'd do well enough. It was not about his health that I was going to trouble you. *Altro !*"

"I can be very patient, signore, especially when I can't help myself. And I must wait as patiently as I can till you are pleased to say what you have to say,—or to allow me to go to my room," said Regina.

"There is no reason for you to be so scornful, signorina; you will see that my news is not such as one would be in a great hurry to speak. The long and the short of it then is this, since you are so pressed for time,—Carlo Caroli has been proved to be a thief! he has done what will send him to the galleys! That is all!"

He had kept his hard bad eyes on her face with a piercing gaze all this time, eagerly waiting for the outburst of emotion, which he doubted not his words would produce. But to his utter surprise, the effect was altogether different from anything he had expected. There was no outburst of emotion of any sort, no word of reply, no change of colour even; no manifestation of anxiety, no symptom of a wish for further details of the startling tidings. But she did look up, proudly raising her small head, and turning it on the magnificent column of her throat towards him, with a look of scorn, so eloquent, so withering, that even Meo Morini understood it, and writhed under it.

He felt as if literally beat down by it for a minute or two. But he recovered the insolent

tone of mind which was natural to him, by an
effort of reflection, which suggested to him, that
it would be really too absurd, that *he* should
permit himself to have the worst of it in such a
conversation as he had come there for.

"All right, *bella signorina!*" he said, "I am
glad that I was mistaken in supposing that it
would matter to you, more than it does to me,
whether the fellow is sent to the galleys or not.
But I am afraid it will vex Signor Bartoli. He
seems to have taken a sort of fancy to the chap,
God knows why. And it's a bad thing for the
widow Monaldi to lose her five hundred dollars
to begin with, and then to have the manager of
her business sent to the galleys. It is not
creditable like to the business. I should say it
would be galleys for life. For robbery by a
confidential and trusted agent from the house of
his employer, is so deuced bad; it shows a
fellow to be such an out and out scamp!"

And all this time the speaker was watching
anxiously, greedily to spy the effect of his words
in the features of his hearer. There was nothing
to be read in those proud cold features, but the

same abiding look of unutterable scorn. But
he could see that she was listening with attention to his words.

"It *is* a bad case, is it not, signorina?" he
said, after a pause, determined to draw some
word from her, and surprised as well as ex-
asperated by her proud silence.

"A very bad case, signore," said Regina,
slowly letting the words fall one by one from
her lips with an expression that seemed as if
her disgust at the person she spoke to communicated itself to the words themselves, and made
them nauseous to her as they passed her lips ;—
"a very bad case, signore, and one which shows
a person to be all you say, that a *man* (with
such an emphasis!) should come with such a
fabrication to a girl under his mother's protec-
tion, rejoicing in the pain which he fancies it
will give her. It is *very* bad!" And she looked
him full in the face with open majestic eyes, as
she said the words.

Again Meo quailed under her look, and under
her words. Still the accusation contained in
them opened to him a possibility of reply, of

which after staggering for a minute under the blow, he hastened to avail himself.

"I am sure, Signorina Regina, I don't know why you should think that I rejoiced, as you say, in telling you of this news, which would have reached you very soon from others, if I had not told you. I thought that it would be a matter of interest to you, and that was what made me come and tell you before any body else. But you *won't* do me justice!"

In her inmost consciousness Regina had no doubt, that her accusation of Meo's malignity was just. She read his heart in this matter, as if it had been an open book before her. She felt that she was not mistaken or unjust. It was nevertheless true, that there was nothing in the words that he had spoken, which could be adduced in proof of the justice of the bitter reproach she had hurled at him. So she replied more quietly, though still with a cold distance of manner, that was little less than repelling.

"Of course, signore, the story you tell, would be a matter of interest to me, if I placed the least faith in it. But I know that it is untrue, and therefore pay no attention to it. May I ask of you, if you believe it yourself?"

"Why, signorina," replied Meo, who felt that he was now once more on vantage ground, "if it was my own father, I could not help believing it, let alone a young man of whom nobody knew anything only a few weeks ago! I am sure I should not have been quick to believe such a thing; it would never have entered into my head! But there is no help for believing it. You will believe it yourself, safe enough, when you have heard the circumstances. It is not a question of suspicion."

"Signore, I shall not believe it," said Regina, quietly but loftily. "I know Signor Carlo Caroli quite well enough to be perfectly certain that he has not been guilty of what you lay to his charge;—quite sure,—absolutely certain of it. Do you not understand that there are persons, of whom it *can not* be true that they are thieves?"

"Well, signorina, you will at least see that I am no quicker to accuse him than all the rest of the world. Everybody will tell you the same;

you will see what your father says about it!"
replied Meo, with a show of plausibility, which
did begin to produce its effect on the mind of
his hearer.

"Innocent men have been suspected before
now!—suspected perhaps by all the world,
except the few who really knew them;" said
Regina, who despite herself was beginning to be
alarmed and uneasy at what she heard. The
colour came into her face, and she could not
prevent herself from feeling anxious to hear
what the terrible circumstances were to which
Meo alluded, though she would have given much
to hear them from any one save him. "I *know*
that Signor Caroli is not a thief!" she repeated,
"although it may be that some unfortunate
circumstances may have caused suspicion in the
minds of people who do not know him."

"Now just you see for yourself, signorina,
whether what I have said is more than the
truth. Just let me tell you the facts of the
case, and then judge whether there is any hope
for him to get out of it. And if I say one word
more than the simple truth, why then never

speak to me again. I can't say fairer than that, can I?" pleaded Meo.

Regina bowed her head without speaking; and then Meo proceeded with lawyer-like conciseness to relate the facts as they had occurred; —the carrying of the money by himself and Simonetti to the widow's house;—Carlo's recommendation that the dollars should be left there, despite of their strongly expressed opinion to the contrary;—the putting of the money in the secret hiding-place of the escritoire;—the discovery that it had been abstracted, as made by himself and Farmer Bratti in company with Caroli himself;—the entire absence of any signs of the escritoire having been meddled with;— Caroli's own spontaneous declaration that the key had been in his keeping ever since the money was placed there;—and, lastly, his own avowal that he was perfectly unable to suggest any possibility of accounting for the disappearance of the money.

Regina sate silent for awhile after Meo had finished his story, deeply thinking. It was evident that he had succeeded at last in

at least awaking her interest, although there
was not the smallest symptom of any of that
emotion, to the witnessing of which he had
looked forward with so much pleasurable
anticipation.

"And what did the widow Monaldi say
about it?" she asked at last.

"Oh, the widow! She made no doubt about
it, that he had taken the money. But she
wanted to make out that he was very welcome
to it. She would be glad enough to say no
more about it, I have no doubt. One understands all *that* very well!" he added, with a
sneer and a leer, which made Regina feel as if
she could have taken him by the throat and
strangled the life out of him then and there.

"If the widow and he had to settle the
matter between them," continued Meo, utterly
unconscious of the feeling he had called forth,
and incapable of comprehending the nature of
it ;—" if it was only the widow and he who had
the settling of the matter between them, I
make no doubt it would go smooth enough.
They would find a way of squaring all accounts

quick enough! But you see, signorina, there
was Farmer Bratti and myself. And of course
I must do my duty. I can't be a party to the
concealing of a robbery. What would father
say? And then there's Bratti! To do Caroli
justice, too, he knew himself that it must all
come out. When we said, naturally enough,
that the matter could not rest there, he said
'No; of course it could not. The case must
be inquired into.' He said so, himself."

"You don't mean to say, that Signor Caroli
admitted that he had taken the money?" said
Regina, with flashing eyes.

"No! Of course he was not going to be
such a fool as to do that. Of course not!
But, signorina," he added, in a tone that was
meant to be at once confidential and insinuat-
ing, "I was thinking, as I came from Sponda
Lunga here,—and that was what made me so
anxious to tell you all about it before it had got
about,—I was thinking, that if you really did
care about it,—merely as an acquaintance, you
know,—to avoid the talk there would be, if one
who had been a rather intimate acquaintance of

yours, one may say,—singing together, and such like,—should be sent to the galleys . . . . if you really did care to have it hushed up . . . . and if you asked me to hush it up . . . . well, surely you know, Signorina Regina, that I could not find it in my heart to refuse you that or anything else," said Meo, leering at her with what was meant to be a look of intense devotion.

"I don't know what you mean!" said Regina, really puzzled from her utter inability to comprehend all the baseness involved in the ideas which this suitor for her hand was endeavouring to make her share with him.

"Why, look here, signorina," he said, with a feeling of being driven to bay, "if any good is to be done in this matter, we must understand one another. It is no good beating about the bush. I'll tell you what it is ;—I *could* hush this matter up! The widow would ask nothing better! And Bratti I could manage. I *could* do it, I say. Now, stop a minute ; hear what I wish to say!" he continued, as he saw an angry look coming across her brow, though she

still had no clear idea of the nature of the
bargain to be proposed to her. "Let us look
at the facts as they are. It is quite out of the
question,—of course you must know that it
is altogether out of the question that . . . .
that . . . . there should be anything between
you, signorina, and this Caroli, after what has
happened. I don't say that anything of the
sort was ever in contemplation," he went on
hurriedly and deprecatingly ; "there is no need
to say whether such a thing was ever thought
of or not. But it is at all events clear, that is
now out of the question for ever. You must
feel that, signorina, yourself. You know, on
the other hand, the devoted attachment with
which I have regarded you ever since I knew
you. I won't go into that at any greater
length, for if we are to understand each other,
time is of value,—and you know all I could say.
Well ! look here,—one word is as good as a
thousand. Just you put that darling little
hand into mine and say, ' Meo Morini, I will be
your wife, if nothing more is heard of this
charge against Signor Caroli,' and I'll engage

that it shall all be made as smooth for him
as oil on beans. Is it a bargain?" and Meo
held out his long, slender, dry hand as he
concluded.

Regina sate silent and motionless. She was
literally struck dumb by the monstrosity, the
cynicism, and the audacity of the man who
dared so to speak to her.

" Why do you suppose," she said presently,
in a low, quiet voice, and without looking at
him ;—" why should you suppose that I should
be so desirous of shielding Signor Caroli from
the consequences of the crime which you
believe him to have committed ?"

" Well, signorina, one does not like to
see one's friends sent to the galleys! *Diamine!* That stands to reason, does it not?"
he said.

" But it is a very high price that you propose
to me to pay for his escape," she replied, in the
same tone and manner.

" You know best about that, signorina," he
rejoined, doggedly. " But I thought that you
did care very much for Signor Carlo, and would

be glad to save him from the galleys,—galleys for life, mind!"

"In short, you thought, and you think, that I love him. Is not that so?" she said, still very quietly.

"And maybe there are others who think that as well as I, signorina! You can't expect people to shut their eyes, or to hold their tongues, for that matter!" said Meo in reply to her question.

"So that your proposal is, that I should promise to marry you because of my love for another man. Is not that your meaning?" said Regina, still without looking up, changing her position, or raising her voice. But any one capable of reading her face would have seen that the storm of suppressed anger and scorn that raged within was rapidly becoming too strong for further suppression. But Meo read nothing, and rushed on to meet his fate.

"Well, signorina, if you will put it so. . . . . But, really now, as the matter stands, what better can you do?"

"Signor Meo Morini!" she said, rising sud-

denly, and speaking as if she were painfully
out of breath, to his great astonishment, while
she confronted him, and looked with upraised
head and widely opened eyes into his face; " I
knew, I have always known that you were . . . .
one to whom no earthly circumstances could
ever have induced me to give my hand or my
heart. But I had no conception that anything
so base and vile had ever breathed the same
air with me. . . . . Go, sir! go! I have one
other word to say. I do love Carlo Caroli! I
am proud to be loved by him! I utterly dis-
believe every word of the vile calumny you
have told me! I have no doubt that his entire
innocence of wrong-doing of any kind will be
abundantly shown. But if he were to be the
victim of a base and wicked conspiracy, not to
save him from the galleys would I add to his
misfortunes the pain of knowing that I had
fallen so low as . . . . as the lot you propose
to me. Now go! go! I will speak with you
no further."

"Very well, signorina! very well! We shall
see what Signor Giovanni will say to all this.

If he likes a galley-slave for a son-in-law . . . .
Padrone! Padronissimo! A rivederla, signorina!" said Meo, eyeing her with intense and
undisguised malignity, as he moved to the
door.

CHAPTER IV.

IT will be readily understood that Meo
Morini was not in a sweet temper, when, feeling
himself compelled to obey Regina's reiterated
commands to "go," he took himself down the
stairs to his father's office. He felt, indeed, as
if all the fiends were unchained and raging
within his bosom. Never had he hated anybody,—and it is saying a great deal; for Meo
was, like most of his countrymen, a good hater,
—never had he hated anybody as he now
hated that proud girl who had scorned him,
baffled him, and humiliated him, but the possession of whom, nevertheless, he still ardently
desired, and whom he would fain have for his
wife to-morrow.

All his calculations and anticipations had

been frustrated and set at naught. None of all
those varied scenes to which he had looked
forward with so much pleasure had been
enacted for his delectation. The truths which
he had told had been disbelieved. The feelings
which he had intended to conceal, had been
seen through. His friendly offices had been re-
jected with scorn and loathing. His enmity had
been defied. This haughty, insolent girl, for
whom he could not help feeling what he called
love, had dared to avow, nay, to boast of her
love for his rival, though that rival was,—or
would soon be,—an inmate of the galleys! and
though he, Meo Morini, was the suitor for her
hand authorised and approved by her parent!
The insolent, audacious, brazen-faced minx!
But he could afford to bide his time. Her
father was on his side, and Farmer Bartoli was
not wont to brook much opposition to his will;
—specially was little likely to brook it on a
question of this sort from his daughter. Oh,
yes! his day would come! And then . . . .
(and Meo smiled a smile that might have
scared a child, or made a good wife cross

herself, as the thought crossed his mind) : . . . .
then, if he did not find the means to tame this
proud spirit, and make her rue the hour in
which she had treated him with scorn,—why,
then, those might laugh that won, that was all!
These thoughts in his heart, his first impulse
was to seek the farmer, and make him the
second recipient of his news.

But Bartoli was still absent with the lawyer.
And Meo, in a state of mind which made it
absolutely impossible to him to remain at rest
while he waited the return of his father and the
farmer, determined to go to his friend, Andrea
Simonetti, and tell him the news. There at
least he was sure of finding a sympathising
auditor. It was an hour at which he should be
pretty sure of finding the usurer's son at his
office, and it was not five minutes' walk from
his own door.

So he went to Simonetti's office, and did find
the young man there, and alone, too, by good
luck, so that he could speak what he had to say
freely.

"Andrea, *caro mio*," he began at once, "I

have a bit of news for you, that I don't think you will be more sorry to hear than I was. But you'd never guess it, not if you were to try from now to Christmas."

"Out with it, then, old fellow! I never guess, except when there is no other way of finding out what I want to know."

"Well, then, what do you think of this? That scamp Caroli, at Sponda Lunga, has been robbing the widow, and been caught as neat as a rat in a trap! I declare I am not sorry for it. It serves the widow no more than right!"

"And I am not surprised at it," answered Andrea. "I never liked that fellow! To my thinking he has the galleys in his face as plain as ever man had. What's the game he's been up to?"

"You remember that five hundred dollars we took over to the widow that night, and the putting it in the secret drawer of the escritoire? Well, as sure as the devil hates holy water, he has nabbed it. And the way he was caught was the neatest thing you ever saw."

"You don't say so! Well, I thought he was

up to something of the kind! I wish I may die if I didn't! Don't you remember, Meo, how we advised the widow not to keep the money in the house, and how nothing would suit him but that it should be left there?" said Andrea, exultingly.

"To be sure I do! I should think I did, too; and am ready to swear to every word of it! He would be responsible for the care of it, he said."

"A pretty sort of responsibility, upon my word! Well, it serves the widow right, it must be owned. Now it is to be hoped she'll see the difference between well-known sponsible people and vagabonds whom nobody ever heard of! How did it come out?"

"Why, this way. It was beautiful. I and Farmer Bratti of Sponda Lunga,—you know who I mean—undertook to collect subscriptions for the people ruined by the flood. Well, we go to the widow of course. She is ready enough,—puts down her name for five-and-twenty dollars. 'But you must call again,' says she, 'for I have not so much by me.' 'Talking of that,' says I, 'what did you find to do with the five hundred dollars?' 'Never thought of it from that day to this,' says she; 'there's the money in the house still. I did not think of that,' says she; 'and I can give you the five-and-twenty dollars out of that, and save your calling again,' says she. So she tells him to go for the money, and he gets up to go for it as bold as brass! 'Have you got the key?' says she. 'It has never been out of my keeping from that day to this,' says he. Think of his being soft enough to admit that!"

"It is always the way with such fellows!" said Andrea. "Seems like as if Providence wanted such things to be found out, and led 'em on to let the cat out of the bag. He lost his head I suppose!"

"Anyway, out he goes as bold as brass, as I said, to pretend to look for the money. And now mark how beautiful we tripped him. I don't know whether it was Providence, as you call it, or the devil put it into my head to re-member the curiousness of the secret hiding-place. 'You never saw a thing of the sort so well managed,' says I to Bratti ; 'with Signora Monaldi's permission,' says I, 'just come in and look at it ; it's worth your while,' says I. So Bratti and I went in to the other room with him. He opens the lock of the escritoire ;—lock all right, mind you !—opens the secret well ;— devil a *soldo* there ! as of course he knew very well, only he had not counted on our being by when he opened it. Was ever a fellow better caught ? "

" Capital, capital ! It's perfect ! There's not a hole for a weasel to wriggle out by ! Well, and how did he take it ? "

" Oh, pretended to be scared, of course !— *was* scared, true enough, for that matter ; but had not so much as a ghost of a word to say for himself. Said he knew nothing about it, of course. But it seemed to me as if he gave up."

" I don't see what else he could do ! It's a clear case if ever there was one. What will it be, Meo ? Galleys for life, I should say."

" I should think so ; I think it must be ! But, Andrea, you have not asked about the widow ! You have not asked how *she* took it !

And to tell you the truth, that seems to me the
part of the case most likely to break down . . . .
if it wasn't for Bratti and me being there."

"Why, what did the widow say?" asked
Andrea, looking up sharply.

"Why, began to say that she did not want
any words about it ;—that he knew he might
borrow the money if he wanted it, and such
like."

"No! you don't mean it!" said Andrea.
"What idiots women are! It *is* lucky that you
and the farmer saw it all as you did. But you
may depend on it, the widow will do nothing,
so far as depends on her, Meo. But I don't
suppose that signifies. Thieves can't get off
that way, I suppose?"

"No, I should say not! I have been thinking a deal about it ; and my notion is, that we
ought not to wait for her to do anything."

"What, give information to the tribunal ourselves?" asked Andrea.

"Simpler than that! Just tell the police
that a robbery has taken place at such a house,
and they are wanted. They don't easily let

go a thing of the kind they have once got hold of."

" Will the police go there for our sending, do you think ? " asked Andrea.

" Well ! I take it they will ; specially, you know, me being a lawyer, and well known. I shall say 'you are wanted directly at such a place ! there has been a robbery of the house ; ' speaking as if I was just come from there, and was bringing them the message like. Of course, they'll suppose that they are sent for by the widow. Oh, yes, they'll be sure to take it up ! Come along with me ! let's go to the police office at once. It's best to lose no time. Who knows whether he may not be off ! "

" Yes, I will go with you ! come along. Certainly, it is best to lose no time. They ought to go out there at once. Come along ! "

So the two friends went to the police bureau, and made their statement to the brigadier.

"I have just come back from the house of a client of ours at Sponda Lunga, Signor Brigadiere, who has been robbed. Some of your people are wanted there in a hurry. We have

got a clear clue to the thief, and if you look
sharp you'll clap your hands on him. It is
Signora Monaldi, the wheelwright's widow, you
know. She has been robbed by her managing
man,—a very bad case of abuse of confidence!
It is five hundred dollars; and the case is as
clear as a pikestaff."

"No! You don't mean that that young
Caroli has robbed his employer!" said the
brigadier. "Why he is come of very decent
people, as I understand! Does he know of the
charge against him?"

"He knows that the money has been missed;"
said Meo, evasively; "and you had better lose
no time, *Signor Brigadiere*. I and this gentleman, Signor Andrea Simonetti, will be important
witnesses in the matter; for the money was
carried from my father to the widow by us;
and we saw it put in the lock-up place, from
which it has been stolen. It is a very ugly
case!"

Five hundred dollars stolen in a dwelling
house by a confidential servant of the person
robbed, was a matter the importance and

interest of which warranted the brigadier in proceeding himself to the investigation of it. So he said he would take a subordinate with him, and get on his horse, and ride off to Sponda Lunga at once.

"Signor Andrea Simonetti, did you say this gentleman was?" asked the brigadier, as the two young men turned to quit the office.

"*Si, Signor Brigadiere;* Signor Andrea Simonetti, of San Michele. He will be able, together with me, to prove the placing of the money in the escritoire, which was in charge of the accused;" replied the young lawyer.

"Oh! I only asked, hearing the name;" returned the brigadier, "because one of our men has gone to look for Signor Simonetti, not ten minutes ago. I make no doubt you will find him waiting for you, sir, if you are returning home now."

"One of your men wanting *me!*" said Simonetti, looking round sharply; "what in the world can any of your people want with me, *Signor Brigadiere?*"

"Oh, only about owning a handkerchief, or

some such article, which has your name on it.
It was sent down to us from Florence. It has
no doubt been stolen from your pocket some
time or other. There's no saying where such
articles mayn't travel to! And very often they
serve as useful clues in our business; besides
that, people like to get their property back
again. Any way, this was sent down by the
police at Florence to be owned. I don't know
any of the particulars of the case. Likely
enough you may be troubled to give evidence."

"I am sure I know nothing of losing any
handkerchief!" said Simonetti, with a certain
amount of uneasiness in his manner.

The brigadier and his subordinate rode off to
Sponda Lunga; and the two young men turned
away together.

"I am sure I don't know what the fellow
means! I have lost no handkerchief!" said
Simonetti, who appeared, to his friend's surprise,
so much amazed at this incident, that it seemed
to occupy his mind to the exclusion for the
moment of that which was so entirely upper-
most in the thoughts of his companion.

"Shall I go home with you, and see what it is about? Perhaps you might want a professional word of advice," suggested Meo.

"No, thank you! No. It can be nothing of any consequence. I'll tell you, if there is any need of a stroke of your trade. Good day, Signor Meo, I won't keep you," and Simonetti turned his face homeward.

Meo had wanted to talk a good deal more about the great event of the morning; and was surprised that his friend, who was, he was quite sure, just as glad as he was himself of Caroli's approaching ruin and disgrace, should be willing to dismiss the subject so quickly.

"I don't know what has come to him!" he muttered, looking after Simonetti, as he strode away; "he seems quite put out about this handkerchief! It *is* a great bore that a man should have his pocket picked first, and then be threatened with all kind of bother about it afterwards! He had better have let me go with him. I know how to tackle those fellows better than he does."

And then he bethought him that he had

still much to do in the matter of the great
Sponda Lunga robbery, and that of a kind that
was very agreeable to him.   He had to tell the
news to his father and Signor Bartoli.   He was
especially anxious to see how the latter would
receive the tidings, and eager to impress on
the farmer's mind a right direction on the
subject at starting.   So dismissing Simonetti
from his thoughts altogether, he hurried home-
wards.

He met Bartoli and his father coming up to
the lawyer's door at the same moment with
himself.

"Have you heard the news, Signor Giovanni?" he cried, as they came up.

"What do you mean?   I've heard no news!
Is there another flood?" replied Signor Bartoli
rather crossly, as he thought.

"Nor you, father! have you been out all day
without hearing it?   *Pare impossibile!*" cried
Meo, with well acted surprise.

"Well! what is it?   Don't stand there
gaping!   I've heard nothing.   What are you
talking about?" said his father.

"Why, there's the devil of a piece of work out at Sponda Lunga! That young fellow Caroli has been robbing Widow Monaldi! the whole of that five hundred dollars you sent her by me,—every penny of it. The police are out there now, and every body is talking of it!"

"Carlo Caroli robbed his employer ;—robbed the widow Monaldi! I don't believe a word of it!" said the farmer.

"Why, Meo, you don't mean it ? Are you sure of what you are saying ? It's best to be cautious in repeating such rumours, *figliuolo mio!*" said the lawyer.

"*I'm* awake, father!" replied his son; "rumours, by Jove! It is no rumour at all! You'll believe it fast enough, Signor Giovanni, before many more hours go over your head!"

"But who did you hear it from ? that's the first question!" said his father, as they all three entered the lawyer's studio together.

"Hear it from! From the parties themselves! I may say I saw it! I did not see him take the money, of course ; but I was there when it was missed. I went out collecting sub-

scriptions for the sufferers by the flood, you
know; I and Farmer Bratti.   Well, we went to
the widow's house first thing in Sponda Lunga, of
course.   She put down her name for five-and-
twenty dollars;—five-and-twenty because she
said it was not for her to put herself on the
same level with father, and father's name is
down for thirty.   So she asks Caroli to go and
get the money from the five hundred that had
been in his keeping.   We saw it put away in a
secret hiding-place, Simonetti and I, and the
widow herself, all saw him stow it away, lock
the place, and put the key in his pocket, which
please to observe, he admits never to have been
out of his keeping since.   Well, he gets up to go
into the next room, where the money was,—and
I and Bratti go with him.   He opens the desk
with the key, all right enough,—opens the secret
place;—devil a rap was there!   Mark too, that
the money had been left there against the advice
of Simonetti and me, because he would have it
so, and overpersuaded the widow.   Of course,
he said he knew nothing about it; but he had
not a word to say in explanation of the disap-

pearance of the cash. And now, Signor Giovanni, what do you think *that* looks like ? And
if you don't believe me, ask Bratti, and he'll tell
you the same story."

"Well!" said the farmer, after a pause, "it
has a very ugly look about it, certainly ; that
can't be denied ! a *very* ugly look ! And I am
very sorry for it. I'd give five hundred dollars
out of my own pocket, rather than this should
have happened. But for all that, Meo, my boy,
don't let us be too much in a hurry. I don't
think that lad is 'a thief. There's all sorts of
accidents may happen. What did the widow
say to it ? "

"Oh, the widow!" said Meo, with a shrug :
"*you* know what women are, Signor Giovanni.
She would ask nothing better than to hush it
up. She said that he knew very well that he
might borrow the money if he wanted it. But
that won't do, you know. One is not going to
see a thief let off in that way ! "

"I'll tell you what, Meo, my fine fellow !"
returned the farmer, while a lowering frown
came over his brow, " it seems to me that it is

more nuts to you than otherwise, that this poor young fellow should have got into this trouble. Now, I don't like the look of that at all; certainly, it's very true, what you say, that the Signora Marta can't wipe it up that way; that's not the way to set his credit and character straight. But hang me, if you don't seem to think it's a capital piece of good news! And *per Dio!* that, to my thinking, is as ugly as any other part of the story. Dash me, if it isn't every bit as ugly!" said the farmer, with a look of disgust, and gathering excitement from his own words as he went on.

Old Morini saw that his son had made a mistake, and hastened to endeavour to repair it.

"I am sure, Bartoli, that we should, all of us, be as sorry as you could be, that this has happened. And Meo would be as much vexed as any of us. I am sure he would ;—though he may seem excited-like by having been present at such a painful scene. Let us hope that some way of proving the young man's innocence may turn up."

"Ah! that's the proper way to look at it!'

said the farmer. "But if the widow wanted to hush it up," he continued, turning to Meo, "how comes it .... did not you say that the police were gone out there now?"

"Yes, they are indeed!" replied Meo, not perceiving at once the drift of the farmer's question.

"But if the widow didn't want no notice taken of it .... " said Bartoli again.

"Well .... as you said yourself, Signor Giovanni, that would not do, you know," answered Meo, colouring up painfully.

"Of course, it wouldn't do to hush it all up! Of course, the matter must be inquired into, and the truth known! But if the widow did not want to make a piece of work, it stands to reason she did not send for the police. Who did? That's what I want to know. Who was in such a devil of a hurry to hound *them* on to the poor fellow's traces?" asked the farmer, who had gradually worked himself into a passion, striking his hand violently upon the lawyer's studio table, as he spoke, and looking angrily at Meo under his lowering brows.

" Who sent the police ? " faltered Meo, " why,
of course, nobody can send them but the magistrates, or their own officers. Why, bless you,
Signor Giovanni, the police,—they .... it's their
business, you know, to look up such things."

"Business or not," persisted Bartoli, "they
can't do their business till they hear of it. How
did they hear of this business out at Sponda
Lunga? They mostly hear of such things by
the people that's robbed sending to tell 'em of
it. But we know that the widow did not send
to 'em at all ! Of course she didn't. Now I
want to know how the police heard anything
about it, within an hour or so after it was found
out ? That's what I want to know ? " repeated
the farmer, standing with his head peering
forward, his hands in his breeches pockets, and
one heavy foot planted firmly in advance, while
he fixed his angry eyes on Meo's crimson down-
looking face.

" Well, Signor Giovanni, there's nothing for
you to be angry about ! Any way, the young
fellow is nothing to you, I suppose, one way or
t'other," whined Meo.

"Never you mind that!" said the farmer, retaining his menacingly interrogatory attitude; "never you mind that! Mayhap he may be, and mayhap he mayn't. I say, I want to know, who sent the police on this here errand out to Sponda Lunga? Who told 'em anything about the job? Answer me that!"

"Well . . . . if you want to know . . . ." hesitated Meo; "Simonetti and I . . . . that is, Simonetti said that he thought . . . . I say, Simonetti . . . ."

"Damn Simonetti!" cried Bartoli; "who told Simonetti anything about it, I should like to know! I say, who told him?"

"Why, I did!" said Meo, striving to rally his courage. "I told Simonetti what I had seen. Why shouldn't I, I should like to know!"

"And then Simonetti runs off, post haste to the police, eh? out of his own head, without waiting to know whether the party robbed made any complaint or not? Was that it, eh?" said the farmer.

"Yes! he went to the police! he thought

it his duty to do so!" said Meo, putting as bold a front on it as he could.

"And, pray did he go alone? Was it master Andrea Simonetti that took it on himself to turn himself into an officer of police? Did he go alone, I say?" asked Bartoli, still in a voice of restrained anger.

"No! we went together for that matter! I did what I thought it my duty to do; and I am not ashamed to say so!" said Meo, with a very unsuccessful attempt to bluster.

"But it seems to me," sneered Bartoli, while the lawyer shuffled uneasily in his great armchair, which stood between the wall and the studio table;—"it seems to me that you are very much ashamed, as well you may be! But I thought you said just now, that the police would not go for the sending of anybody, barring of course the people whose house had been robbed. How came they to go for your sending?"

"Well, they knew that I had just come from the place, and . . . ."

"Oh! they knew that!" interrupted the

farmer; . . . . "not without your telling them, I suppose! Ugh!" and Bartoli prolonged the exclamation into a sort of hoot, with such an expression of intense disgust in it, as only an Italian can throw into it.

The fact was, that Meo had been playing a part, which, mean and detestable as it must appear to anybody able to read his motives, was especially so to an Italian, and yet more especially to an Italian of the *contadino* class. The law has for so many generations been recognised in Italy as the oppressor rather than as the protector of the people, that none of its operations have their sympathy. And in the country this feeling is especially strong. A man is rarely willing to call on the law to avenge his own wrongs;—thinks that worse will be in some way likely to come of it, if he should do so. And it may be imagined, therefore, with what sort of feeling a man would be regarded, who made himself an amateur carrier of information to the police in a case when the person aggrieved had shown no disposition to call on the law in the matter. To which may

E 2

LIBRARY
UNIVERSITY OF ILLINOIS

be added a very tolerably clear comprehension
on the part of the farmer of the nature of Meo's
motives.

"Look, Morini," he said, turning to the old
lawyer, after he had given expression to his
loathing in the manner that has been described;
"look what this fellow has been doing! As
soon as ever he had the chance to light upon
this unhappy business he comes back to Lucca
hot-foot and posts away to the police, giving
them to understand that he is come as a messenger from the widow. I see it all plain
enough. And I understand all about it too!
Why should he be in such a hurry to be down
on this young man? Because he hates him!
Why does he hate him? Because he thinks
that mayhap this Caroli stands in his way with
my daughter! Do you think I don't see it all?
Why, man, we country folks have got eyes in
our heads as well as others!"

"But surely, Signor Giovanni," whined Meo,
"you wished that I should have the honour,—the
great honour—of the Signorina Regina's hand!
Surely I had your approbation! And . . . ."

" Yes, Signor Meo ; it is true ! I did wish it ! I thought that it would be a good match for my girl. Signor Morini, here, is my old friend. I had never heard anything against you. I thought that it would be putting money to money ; and that it would do well for both sides . . . ."

" Well then ! . . . ." said Meo half crying, " wasn't I right to . . . . just you speak to *la Signorina* Regina ! See what she'll say ! Why she told me to my face to-day, that she loved this fellow Caroli ! If she didn't I wish I may never break bread again ! And wasn't I right to go the best way to put a stop to that ? I suppose you don't want the Signorina Regina to marry a known thief, do you ? "

" No, sir ! " cried the farmer, now purple in the face with passion, and striking his open palm heavily on the table by the side of which he was standing, while his deep-set eyes gleamed dangerously ;—" No ! sir ! my daughter will not marry a thief ! but I'm damned if she shall marry an informer ! "

CHAPTER V.

It was about an hour since Farmer Bartoli, after speaking the words recorded at the end of the last chapter, had left the studio and gone upstairs, minded to ascertain from his daughter the truth of Meo's assertion, as to what she had said to him, and whether he had yet communicated to her the story of Caroli's crime— or misfortune. The lawyer and his son had remained there together during this time, which had been passed in close conversation between them. Meo had had to endure during the first part of this time, many reproaches from his father, as to his imprudence in managing to get into such a terrible mess with the farmer. It was in vain that he pointed out to his father the danger of having that Caroli in his path, and the great desirability of getting him well out of it, for good and all.

"But there was no need to let him see how glad you were, specially when you saw how he took to the fellow the other day after that business the night of the flood. And above all, there was no need to act as if you were a common police informer, and then to let him know it. You might have trusted to his not giving Regina to a man under strong suspicion of being a common thief. There was no use in being in such a hurry in the matter. But that's what young people always are! We must see if we cannot bring him round a little at supper presently. It is pretty nearly supper time."

"Try you, what you can do, father!" said Meo, who shrunk from meeting the farmer, and especially from meeting Regina at the evening meal; "you will do it better without me! I shan't come up to supper. Better not! It will be time for me to try and come round him, when his passion has gone down a little, and specially when this fellow shall be convicted of theft."

" You really think he took the money then ? "
said his father.

" Really think so ! why of course he took it,
and no mistake ! The case is as clear as
running water ! " said Meo with some contempt
for what seemed to him his father's slowness of
comprehension.

" Well now, Meo, between ourselves," said
the old lawyer, slowly taking a pinch of snuff,
" my notion of that Caroli is that he is not
likely to be a thief. And there's more ways of
getting at the inside of a locked desk than one.
There's one thing, however, which may go a
good way towards catching the thief. It so
happens oddly enough that I can identify any
one of those five hundred dollars I sent by you
to the widow. I had them from that old crack-
brained Spontini, who lives at Ripafratta,—the
old miser, you know ! He has a mania for
marking all the coin that comes into his hand.
I know his mark, and can swear to it. The
thief, whoever he is, little guesses that it is all
marked money ! . . . . See who that is at the
door, Meo ! somebody knocked."

Meo opened the door and admitted the brigadier, who had been at his instigation on the expedition to Sponda Lunga.

"Well, *Signor Brigadiere*," said Meo, bringing him into the studio, "have you caught him? Have you brought the fellow back with you, eh?"

"Brought him back! Signor Morini? no, to be sure not! How could we bring him back when there is no charge made against him! I understood from you that you came from the widow Monaldi, to lodge her complaint. She says that she never made any complaint at all!— that it is all right, and she's quite content; and wants to know who has got anything to say against that!"

Meo and his father looked at each other rather foolishly.

"Seems to me, Signor Morini," said the brigadier after a pause, "that you have sent us on a fool's errand!"

"Why, the fellow himself, he that stole the money, don't deny that it has been taken out of the house, and out of the desk that he has had

the key of all the time in his own keeping!"
said Meo.

"Yes! he says all that himself; and says
that the matter must be looked into;" said the
brigadier; "but that's one thing and going to
nab a man accused of a robbery is another
thing! How was I to put my hand on him,
when the lady that has been robbed says that
she is quite sure it was not he that did it?"

"But at all events it is a case for you to look
into," put in the old lawyer; "it is very clear
that a robbery has been committed."

"Yes, there has been a robbery; and we
know our duty, Signor Morini, without being
sent riding out to Sponda Lunga to look like fools
when we got there;" retorted the officer, who
was somewhat cross at having been excited into
unusual activity by a representation of the state
of the case which turned out to be incorrect.

"Well, I have something to tell you, *Signor
Brigadiere*, which may help to make up for
your needless ride, and be of use to you in
looking into this matter," said old Morini.
"Every one of the stolen dollars was marked.

I paid them over myself to the widow ; and
they came to me from a man who always marks
all the cash that passes through his hands.
Queer fancy, isn't it ? but may turn out useful
sometimes. I know his mark, and can swear
to it."

"Ah ! *that* looks something more like than
sending men scouring the country for nothing,"
said the brigadier. "If you could tell me,
signor, or better still, show me the mark those
dollars had on them, it may be you'd be doing
a good bit towards the catching of the
thief."

"That I can do, and will with pleasure," said
the lawyer ; "for I've some more of the same
lot of dollars by me."

He got up from his chair as he spoke, and
going to an iron safe let into the wall, took
from it a small canvas bag of coin. "Look
here, *Signor Brigadiere*," he continued, taking
one of the dollars from the bag, and pointing
out a minute mark at a particular point in the
device on the coin, "every one of those dollars
will be found to have that mark in the same

place. Here, you keep this one by you. It may be of use to compare others to."

"Thank you, Signor Morini! It is very important. You may depend on it, signor, we will spare no pains to ferret this out. And by the help of this piece of money, I think we have a very good chance. So good evening, gentlemen! *Levo l'incommodo!*" said the officer, using as he left the room the form of speech prescribed by Tuscan courtesy for such occasions, which consists in assuming that your presence must have been a bore to the person you are taking leave of.

"You see, Meo! You were too much in a hurry;—too much in a hurry! Why, you must have known that he could not touch Caroli, if the widow refused to make any charge against him!" said the senior.

"Well, I wanted to speak to you first, to ask you what was best to be done," pleaded Meo; "but I could not find you. I came here first thing, on coming back from Sponda Lunga; but you were out. And I did not want to lose any time. Of course not! Of course I wanted to trounce the fellow. Lord bless you, he stole the money! You may take your oath of that!"

"Yes! but my taking my oath to it would not suffice under the circumstances to fix the fact on him. I am afraid not . . . . under the circumstances. But I think . . . . I think that if he is the thief he'll be nabbed. Yes, I think so! But it is very vexatious that you should have got into such a scrape with Bartoli;—very vexatious."

"Well, it was not my fault!" said Meo somewhat sulkily. "He is such a blunder-headed cantankerous old blockhead!"

"You won't come up? It is supper time!" said his father.

"No! I'd better not! You'll be able to smooth him down better without me. You lay it on thick on me for being hand over head, and incautious, and so angry that the widow should be wronged, and all that; but no more malice in me than a sucking dove! only too glad to see Caroli out of the mess, if he can clear himself honourably, and that sort of thing. You'll do it better without me."

" Very well ! " said his father.   And perhaps
to impress upon any human being an idea that
Meo Morini was moved to generous indignation
by the spectacle of wrong-doing, but had not
an ounce of malice in his composition, *was* in
some degree a less desperate task in his absence, than it would have been while his face
was present as a commentary on the text.

"I shall go and get a bit of supper with
Simonetti.   He feels no doubt at all about
Carlo's guilt."

" Humph !   I should not think *his* opinion
on the matter would be worth much !   Good
night ! "

And with that the father went upstairs to
meet his family and his guests at the supper
table ; and Meo lounged towards the house of
his friend.

But Meo was not destined to pass a pleasant
evening that day !   He did not find his friend
at all in a humour to enjoy the feast of reason
and flow of soul.   Andrea had seemed annoyed
to a degree that his friend Meo did not understand by that matter of the handkerchief to be

owned, of which the police-officer had spoken; and he found him still chafing under it.

"Well! did you find the fellow with the handkerchief when you got home?" asked Meo, on meeting his friend.

"Yes! damn him! he was here waiting for me, sure enough. And he had a handkerchief with my name at full length on it. But there are other people of the name of Simonetti, I know, at Leghorn, and in plenty of other places too, for all I know or care. So why should I own the handkerchief? I said it wasn't mine; I had lost no handkerchief, and knew nothing about it! Why should I go and run my head into I don't know what botheration for the sake of a handkerchief?"

"To be sure! why should you? No good could come of it; and trouble might come. Far better to say at once you knew nothing about it," acquiesced Meo.

"Of course! But there was my sister down in the office by chance at the time. I wish to God women would not come where they have no business! They are always making mis-

chief! So what must she do, like a cursed
fool, but put her oar in, when I said the handkerchief was none of mine, and swear that it
was! 'Oh! Andrea,' says she, 'it *is* yours.
Don't you know it? I can swear to it any day.
For I marked it with my own hands, and
there's others in the house now belonging to
the same set!' says she. Damn her stupid
tongue! I could have knocked her teeth down
her throat with a wipe of my hand, with all
the pleasure in life! Of course I could do
nothing but look foolish. And there stood the
cursed fellow looking hard at me between the
eyes."

"What did you say?" asked Meo sym-
pathisingly.

"Say! What could I say? I said I supposed it must be mine; that I never knew my
own things; and it was women's business to
look after such matters! But I didn't like it a
bit, I tell you."

"Of course you didn't! It was not pleasant.
But after all, the worst that can happen will be
that you should have to make a journey to

Florence to give evidence! Oh! hang the handkerchief! Did the police fellow leave it, or carry it away with him?" asked Meo.

"He wouldn't leave it;—said his orders were to keep possession of it. It was needed for the purposes of justice. Damned nonsense!" said Andrea, evidently much annoyed.

"To be sure it's nonsense. Those fellows always want to make a mountain out of a molehill! It is their trade. I dare say you will never hear anything more about it; and they will keep the handkerchief for their pains!" said Meo.

"So they may and welcome, if they don't bother me any more about it! Damn them! What did your father and Bartoli say to our friend Signor Caroli's job, eh?" asked Simonetti.

"Say! There's all the fat in the fire with that old fool Bartoli! What do you think of his sticking to it that Caroli never took the money, and blowing me up sky high for not being of the same opinion! You should have seen the passion he put himself into!"

"Ah! that is all because of that fellow hauling his daughter through the water at the time of the flood. Don't you remember how he went on about it that morning? But it won't matter much what he thinks about the matter when once master Caroli is safe lodged in the galleys."

"Well, I don't know! He said just now that I was an informer, and swore till he was black in the face that his daughter should not marry such an one! I thought the old fellow would have choked himself, he was in such a passion."

"Never mind! He'll cool down when he sees that you are right, and Caroli is under lock and key! Did you tell the young lady about it?" said Andrea, with a tone and expression that it would have been very unsafe to have spoken of Regina in to Carlo Caroli, but which did not seem in any degree to displease her other lover.

"Yes, I did! And she went on worse than her father;—wouldn't believe anything against him;—told me to my face she loved him, and went on like a mad woman! If ever she *does* come to be my wife . . . . " added Meo, with an expression of diabolical malice impossible to describe, finishing his broken sentence only by pressing his thin white lips firmly together, and slowly nodding his head two or three times to his companion.

"Ye . . . s!" answered Andrea, nodding in return, and with a look of extreme satisfaction in his face; "it is pleasant to be paid when your debtor has run a long score, thinking that pay-day would never come!—very pleasant! I wonder what those police fellows did out there at the widow's?"

" Did? Nothing at all! The brigadier came to our house not an hour ago; and *he* was as cross as two sticks because he said he had been sent on a fool's errand. The widow declared that she had no charge to make against him. And he could not be touched!"

"Damn her, for a fool! But the police can't let such a matter rest. They must look into it; mustn't they?" said Andrea.

"Oh, yes! they must look into it, of course

they will. The brigadier said as much. And by a queer chance father was able to give them a clue that's very likely to be useful. Every one of the dollars we took over to the widow was marked by a man my father had them from."

"Marked, were they?" said Andrea, with a sharp and quick look from under his eye-brows at his companion.

"Yes! every coin of them. And father luckily had some more of the same lot by him, and lent the brigadier one of them and showed him the mark. He said that in his judgment that would go a long way towards running our man down," said Meo.

"Oh! he thought so, did he?" said Andrea, with another quick, covert, and, one would have said, almost alarmed sort of look.

"Yes! and father thought so too! Depend upon it they will be down upon him. And Bartoli can't stand by him then. He can't give his daughter to a man convicted of robbery in the house of his employer. And he'll come round when he remembers how many *scudi* father can put down the day we are married. Oh! He knows which side his bread is buttered. Let Farmer Bartoli alone for that. And then we shall see if the Signorina Regina will kindly tell me again that she loves this galley-slave thief!"

Andrea forbore to interrupt the flow of his friend's pleasing meditations for awhile. He sat biting his nails, and apparently buried in thought. At last he said suddenly—

"I don't know why you should have been in such a confounded hurry to run to the police! What did we need of the police? Would it not have been quite enough to blast his character? Could the widow for very decency sake have kept him in his situation? Could the farmer have let him come near his daughter? Of course he couldn't. It would have been much better to let the police alone."

"I don't see that at all, Andrea! The widow would have never said a word; or made any charge against him! The police would never have taken it up at all! Now, sooner or later, he'll be run down; you see if he isn't!"

"Damn running him down!" growled Andrea, after a pause, during which he still sat
biting his nails and ruminating.

He was evidently not his usual self. Meo
did not know what to make of it. It was
clear that his friend was not in a sociable
humour, or disposed to be good company in
any way. So he decided to "*levare l'incommodo*;" and returning home, crept very quietly
to his chamber, pausing as he passed to listen
whether there were still voices in the room
where the family supped. But all was still;
and Meo went to bed more doubtful whether
his day had been altogether a well-spent one
than he had been a few hours earlier in it.

CHAPTER VI.

GREEK MEETS GREEK.

WHEN, several hours after his usual time, the
Rev. Pasquale Mommi signified to his faithful
housekeeper that he thought he would get up,
despite the indisposition which had prevented
him from arising at his ordinary hour, he found
himself much in need of a little solitary medi-
tation. The tidings of the widow Caroli's
death that morning caused sundry questions
difficult of solution to present themselves for
his urgent consideration. In some respects it
was fortunate enough. If she had not spread
abroad the news of her sudden wealth, she
never could do so more. All risks from that
quarter were made safe. But there was Sibilla!
The widow had very distinctly stated that the
housekeeper knew of the fact of her having

won this stupendous prize. What line was he
to take with regard to the Signora Sibilla?

It was a very difficult question. In the first
place, he made no doubt that the secret remained in the keeping of Sibilla herself. He
knew her, and the sort of motives that would
be likely to actuate her, sufficiently well to feel
very well assured on this point. But Sibilla
knew that the deceased widow had had ten
thousand dollars in her house at the time of
her death, or, at least, on the evening of the
day preceding it. Doubtless she would search
for it, and would not find it. What would
she do thereupon? Give it up, and say no
more about it! Hardly! When she had
satisfied herself that absolutely the money was
not in the house, she would speak to others
about it;—probably in the first instance, to him
himself. And he would, of course, be obliged
to set on foot all the proper means of inquiry
into the circumstances.

Suppose, on the other hand, he were to confide the real facts to his housekeeper? No
human being save his housekeeper and himself

would then know anything about the ten
thousand dollars. They might be appropriated as easily and safely as if they had been
legitimately come by. And there would be no
further trouble or anxiety about the business.

But then the Rev. Pasquale Mommi and his
faithful housekeeper and cousin, the Signora
Sibilla Gralli, know each other very well indeed! And the priest felt, with the most
perfect conviction of not being in danger of
making any mistake upon this branch of the
question, that to confide his secret to Sibilla
would in fact amount to making her the mistress of the ten thousand dollars—ay! and of
himself too! Even if he were to make so great
an effort as to propose to her to divide the
great prize with him, share and share alike, he
knew but too well that no such bargain would
bind Sibilla;—that the half would only whet her
appetite for more, and that his position would
render it impossible for him to refuse her any
demands,—on that subject or on any other!
That respectable citizen and jeweller in Florence, her brother, would also doubtless in such

a case be admitted to his sister's counsels.
The Rev. Pasquale Mommi had in past years
had occasion to know something of Signor
Stefano Gralli.   And the recollection of those
passages in his life did not at all help to make
the notion of such relationship between him
and Signor Stefano Gralli, as would be involved
in the foregoing supposition, tolerable to him.
No! it would never do to make a confidante
of Sibilla!   Better to take the money to the
authorities at once, and say that the deceased
woman had deposited it with him to take
care of.

But the Rev. Pasquale Mommi could not
think that it had come to that pass yet.   In
fact, what was needed more than that he
should carefully keep his own counsel?   The
Signora Sibilla would, as soon as she was convinced that she could not find the money, noise
abroad the fact of the widow having had such
a sum in her possession.   Well!   What then?
There were plenty of possibilities by which its
disappearance might be accounted for.   The
widow might have become uneasy at having so

large a sum in the house, and might have hid it heaven knows where ;—out in the forest, perhaps ;—and very likely gone out for that very purpose, when she fell on the churchyard steps. Or the money might have been stolen. Who was to say what might have happened during the hours of that night, when there was no living creature in the widow's house, or during those morning hours, when the poor woman lay dying, and many persons did come freely into the house, and anybody might have come ?

Clearly, thought the Rev. Pasquale Mommi, this latter was the course for him to pursue ; —say nothing ; and let all inquiry about the money be made to any extent Sibilla and the widow's heirs might choose. And on this course the priest, without much misgiving, decided.

Sibilla had on her side given a passing thought to the expediency of confiding the secret of the ten thousand dollars to the priest. But she had dismissed it almost as soon as it had occurred to her. Why should she do so? If she could not find the money, he would not

be able to do so ! She did not see that he
could help her. To tell him might do harm,
and could do no good. So Sibilla also decided
on keeping her own counsel.

She had spent some hours that morning,
after telling the priest of the widow's death,
alone in the house with the corpse of the dead
woman, engaged in a persevering search for
the money. She had ransacked indefatigably
the entire house. Nevertheless, she was not
yet satisfied. She thought she *knew* that the
money must be there hidden away somewhere ;
and she was very anxious for time and opportunity to make more thorough examination of
the house. She was obliged, however, to return to the Parsonage before the priest's dinner
time.

"Why, Sibilla," he said, when she came, "I
thought you were never going to give me my
dinner to-day ! Where have you been all the
morning ? "

"Well, looking after that poor soul's things
a little, your Reverence ; and shutting the house
up! There's nobody to look after anything.

And all there is in the house might be stolen if I had not locked the place up."

"Very true, Sibilla! Not that I suppose there could be much to steal! They were very poorly off, the Carolis, I take it."

"Yes! they were poor enough! Still, there is something in the house."

"True! And there is no knowing whether there may not have been picking and stealing there already, when the doors were open for anyone to come in that liked. I must write at once to young Caroli to let him know of his mother's death, and tell him he had better come and look after things."

"Do you think it is worth while to do that, your Reverence? It would be putting him to the cost of a journey for next to nothing. Don't you think that we had better see if we can't do what little is necessary for him?" said Sibilla.

"I should not like to make any offer of the kind!" said the priest. "Of course I must write and tell him of his mother's death. He will do as he thinks best about coming here.

If he asks us to do anything for him, it will be
time enough to think about it. There's the ex-
penses of the poor woman's funeral. I suppose
he would not wish his mother to be buried like
a pauper! Something should be done, too, for
her soul. To think of her dying that way
without the sacraments, like a dog. Why was
I not sent for?"

"Why, who in the world dreamt of her
going off like that, and she with nothing the
matter with her, that anyone knowed of!
There was not a soul there, your Reverence,
that had any more idea that she was near her
end than that I am at this present speaking,
God forgive me for saying so!"

"Poor woman! poor woman!" said the
priest. "I will write to Signor Caroli as soon
as I have had my dinner."

The priest's letter was written and sent
down to Pescia that evening, but too late for
the afternoon train; so that it reached Lucca
only the next morning; and was not sent out
to Sponda Lunga till so late in the day that it
reached Carlo's hands very shortly after the

police officers sent out there by Meo Morini had left the widow Monaldi's house on their return to Lucca.

Poor Carlo! He felt, indeed, on reading the few lines in which the priest announced to him the loss of his remaining parent, that misfortunes never come single! The gentle widow was on this occasion also kind as ever, urging him by all means to take a few days' holiday and go to Uzzano. It would be more satisfactory in every point of view that he should do so. And the change would do him good.

" And by the time you come back, dear Signor Carlo, I dare say it will be found out who stole this bothersome money ; and all will come right ! "

" They will say that I am running away because I can't face the accusation. And, besides, I wanted to see that police officer again, and to see other people, and try whether something can not be done towards getting some clue to the manner in which the money was stolen."

"Oh, you may trust to them to do that!" said the widow ; " and as for anybody thinking that you are running away, let me alone to tell 'em where you are gone, and what for, and when you are coming back again, and that you don't mean to rest till you have found out the thief. You must go, Signor Carlo ! "

So it was settled that he should start on his journey to Uzzano,—the second sad pilgrimage he had made thither within so short a time !—the following morning.

Despite all the widow could say, however, and notwithstanding the sacred nature of the call which took him away, it was with great reluctance that Carlo made up his mind to quit the scene of such an accusation as that which weighed on him. And when he had taken leave of the widow for the night, under the understanding that he was to start for Uzzano by daylight the next morning, and he sate himself down in his chamber before going to bed, to think once more ; he could not make up his mind to go away without explaining, at least to one person, the cause of his absence.

It will be readily imagined that the one person in question was no other than Regina.

Yet he felt considerable reluctance to write to her. He had never yet done so; and though that had passed between them which was enough to more than justify him in doing so. Yet all that, as he bitterly said to himsélf, was under other and very different circumstances. That was when no cloud rested, or ever had rested on his name! Now all was very different! Was it right—was it generous to choose this moment to claim the love which had been promised to him when all was so different? Yet, again, on the other hand, it surely was due to Regina that he should at least tell her that the charge brought against him was vilely false. Yes! that at least he owed to himself and to her. Yet, to tell her,—to tell Regina that in reality he was not a thief! It was too humiliating! Yet again, to be silent under the charge;—and to go away in silence! He could *not* bear that.

So he took a sheet of paper and placed himself at his table, pen in hand.

But the difficulties of his task presented themselves on the very threshold of it. How should he
address her? The all-embracing English "Dear,"
—"Dear Miss Bartoli," —" *Cara* Signorina Bartoli," was of course out of the question. No man
save a husband or privileged lover may address
a lady as " *Cara*." "*Carissima* "—" dearest "—
is oddly enough to our notion perfectly permissible. It may be used to any lady with whom
the writer is on tolerably intimate terms of
acquaintanceship. But neither did this please
Carlo in the present case. If the "*Cara*" was
more than he dared to venture on, the " *Carissima*" was less than he felt he was entitled to.
It was too "*banale*,"—too unmeaning ; the tone
of easy acquaintanceship which did not aspire
or seek to be more. At last he determined on
seeking refuge in that pretty form of Tuscan
courtesy, which, while custom made it what any
gentleman might address to any lady, did at
the same time seem to him to express what was
specially due to her he loved.

"*Gentilissima* Signorina Regina," he wrote,
and then paused again. It was not that he did

not know quite well what he wanted to say;
but a thousand doubts arose as to the shade of
interest that he ought to assume, that she
might feel on the subject of his sorrow and disgrace. He sat gazing at the words he had
written, and letting his mind wander to the
visions and emotions which they called up; till
the village clock striking ten reminded him that
the hours were running away, and that he must,
if the letter were to be written at all, apply himself at once to write it. Thinking had advanced
him no further than he had been when he sat
down to write. So he determined to trust to
the unstudied inspiration of his heart, and give
the reins to his pen :—

"Sponda Lunga.

"Gentilissima Signorina Regina,—It is but
a very short time,— you will perhaps remember
how short,—since I was called away to my home
by the death of my father. I have to-day received a letter from Uzzano, informing me of
the sudden death of my mother ! And I must
go thither to bury her. I start hence to-mor-

row morning. I must suppose that you have
heard of circumstances which make it very painful to me to absent myself from this place at
the present time. You have heard, doubtless,
that I am charged with having robbed my kind
employer, the widow Monaldi, of a large sum of
money. I will not waste any of the few minutes
I have in telling you, Signorina Regina, that I
did not do this thing. For it would not be
proper for me to write to you at all, if I supposed that you could believe me guilty of it.
The assurance that you can not, and do not
believe it, is an immense consolation to me.
And it is the only consolation I have under
the very terrible misery that has fallen upon
me. For I cannot conceal from myself, or from
you, Signorina Regina, that others, very nearly
all others, will believe that I am a thief, and a
thief of the basest and vilest sort. It is a certain fact that the money, five hundred dollars,
has been stolen. It is certain that it was placed
in a special secret drawer of a secretary in the
presence of several witnesses, I myself being
one of them. It is certain that the money,

when sought for to-day, was found to be missing. And it is certain that the key of the secretary has been in my keeping all the intervening time. It is true, also, most unfortunately, that the money was deposited in the place in question, instead of being left in the hands of Signor Meo Morini, by my advice. Under such circumstances, who will believe that I did not touch it;—that I do not know and cannot guess by what means it has been abstracted? The Signora Monaldi herself at first believed that I must have taken the money, though she was generously eager to make no charge against me on that account. I have I trust succeeded in inducing her to believe that I am entirely ignorant and innocent on the subject. But I cannot expect similarly lenient judgment from those who do not know me, or from those who, knowing me, are prejudiced against me. In the eyes of the public around us, Signorina Regina, I stand a convicted thief! Can you not form some notion of the agony with which I feel this and write it, from the tone of this letter! It was not thus that I spoke to you

when last—oh, merciful Heaven! for the last
time, in all human probability,—I spoke to
you! I pressed you to my heart, and called
you my Regina; and you told me that you
were mine! Great God! how long the interval
seems from that time to this! It would be the
height of insolent audacity to call you so now!
It would be the basest ingratitude to make what
has been, and is gone for ever, an excuse for
seeking to drag you within the circle of infamy
that must close around my name. Oh, Regina!
my Regina once, do not believe that if I could, I
would mitigate my own misery by allowing you
to share it, or your name to be sullied by the
disgrace that has fallen upon mine. But I
entreat you to believe that, whatever future may
be before me, the love I bear you will be my
heart's ruling passion till it beats no longer, and
that the remembrance of the love you once gave
me will be the only precious memory of my life!

"Adieu, Regina! Do not write to me;—it
might compromise you to do so. But if you
can honestly say that you are sure that I did
not do this infamous thing, it would be the only

comfort that I am capable of receiving. You might find an opportunity of saying as much to the widow Monaldi.

"I have been rather at a loss how to send this letter to you. I have at last determined to ask old Caterina to take it to you. I will call at the blacksmith's cottage, where she still is finding a shelter, as I walk into Lucca to-morrow morning, and give it to her.

"I am, *gentilissima Signorina*, no more yours, but misfortune's own, in great distress and misery of heart,

"CARLO CAROLI."

It was late in the night before Carlo had finished this letter, by far the longest, as well as the most difficult, he had ever written. He closed and sealed it; addressing it,—

> " Alla gentil^{ma} Signora
>> " La Signorina Regina Bartoli,
>>> " S.B.M."

" To the gentle lady, the demoiselle Regina

Bartoli, her fair hands," the S.B.M. standing for
" *Sue belle mani.*"

The next morning he started with the earliest
dawn on his walk to Lucca ; and calling at the
Ripalta blacksmith's cottage on the way, found
no difficulty in inducing Regina's old servant,
Caterina, to take the letter, and charge herself
with the task of placing it in the young lady's
own hands.

CHAPTER VII.

OLD Caterina performed her promise faith-
fully. But by the time Regina was reading
Carlo's letter, the latter was already pushing his
way up the paved mountain road through the
chestnut woods that leads from the valley to
Uzzano. The railway had brought him as far
as Pescia, but the remainder of the journey had
to be performed on foot. His last walk that
way had been a sufficiently melancholy one, yet
he had not on that occasion carried with him
the terrible weight of hopeless misery that now
made his footstep heavy and his brow dark.
Hopeless,—or nearly hopeless! For what hope
could there be for him save in the detection of
the real thief whose deed was so inevitably im-
puted to him ? He was quite aware that he had

nothing to fear from the pursuit of the law. The law *might* help him, if it could succeed in discovering and showing by what agency the widow Monaldi's money had been abstracted. But in the face of her declaration that she had no charge to make against him, and utterly disbelieved that he had anything to do with the robbery, the police of course could not molest him. But there was very small comfort to be found in this. His character was gone! He was generally believed to be the basest of thieves. Throughout all his little world he was and would be infamous! Enough in itself to bring a high and noble spirit very low! But had this been all, there might still have been a remedy. There were other lands where a good conscience and a brave heart might have found a fair field open to them. But what could he care for any future, or for any hope, the first condition of which was the loss of Regina. And in his letter he said no word more than he fully meant and felt. He truly thought that all hope, all possibility was over for him as regarded his love.

Wearily he plodded on up the steep path, carrying the weight of these bitter thoughts, till he came to the zig-zag in the path, from which the house of his parents, as was said in a former page, was visible. And the spot turned the current of his musings into another channel. He thought of the old days when he had so often paused there to look at the light gleaming from the well-known window, and of the kind faces and loving hearts that had been waiting there to greet him on his arrival. There was no light now. The loving hearts were gone! All was gone!

He set his face to the hill-side and plodded wearily on.

The priest's letter had told him that his housekeeper had taken it upon herself to lock up the house, and that he would find the key at the Parsonage, if he would call there as he passed on entering the village. He was about to do so, therefore, had he not met the Signora Sibilla, evidently on the look-out for him, soon after he passed under the ruinous gateway of the town.

"Ah, Signor Carlo!" she said, "I thought it was about the time for you to get here. I thought that you would take the morning train. Well, I am right glad that you have come! 'Sibilla,' your poor dear blessed mother, *buon' anima sua*, says to me one day, 'Sibilla, you are the only friend I have, now that my beloved husband has gone to a better world, and Carlo has gone to Lucca; and if anything should happen to me,' she says, 'you'll be the one that Carlo will look to, to see all's done as should be. You and he,' says she, 'will see to what little there is left behind me!' And little did I think that her words would come true so soon. Well, well! it is the way we must all go! In the midst of life we are in death! See, here's the key of the house. I will go and show you where everything is."

"Need I give you that trouble, Signora Sibilla? I doubt not that I shall find everything has been well cared for. Can I not go by myself?" said Carlo, who was very anxious to get rid of his companion.

"No!" said Sibilla; "let them that locks

open! I must give up the place to you regular.
Besides, Signor Carlo," she said, dropping her
voice to a whisper, and walking closer by his
side, " there is something else ;—something
very particular, that you don't know, and that I
must tell you about. But I can't speak here in
the street,—wait till we are inside the house."

" Would it not do to-morrow morning, Signora
Sibilla ? " said Carlo, who looked forward with
dread to this woman's presence with him in the
desolate house, and would have given much to
escape from her.

" Not by no means ! " returned Sibilla, very
decisively ; " not by no means ; and so you'll
say, when you come to hear what I have got to
say. There, take the key, and open the door,
and let's get in out of the street, and I will tell
you something as will make your ears tingle ! "

Carlo groaned in spirit and resigned himself
to the infliction, which he saw no means of
escaping.

As soon as they were inside the house, Sibilla
led the way directly to the little closet which
has been described, as having been his father's

special place of retirement, and from which the crucifix had been taken. When they entered the small space, Sibilla pointed to the wall, and asked him if he missed anything that ought to have been there.

" I think," said Carlo, " that there used to be a crucifix hanging on that wall ! I think that I remember it, but I am not sure. Everything else seems to be just as I have so often seen it . . . . just the same."

" Yes, there was a crucifix there ! And you might ask, you know, what has become of it ? And it would be my duty to tell you. Your blessed mother took that crucifix from the wall and sold it in Florence ! "

" Ah ! poor mother ! It was well there was anything she could sell. She must have been hard pressed enough ! "

" Ah, but the Signora Barbara, *buon' anima*, would never have sold that crucifix, let it ha' been how it would, but for a special reason ! "

And then she told him all about the dream, —the sale of the crucifix by means of her re- commendation to her brother, who had given the immense sum of twenty-seven dollars for it,—and the purchase of the lottery-ticket, and the prize.

" Do you mean to say, Signora Sibilla, that my mother received a sum of ten thousand dollars but a few days ago ? " asked Carlo, in amazement.

" I do mean to say so, and I saw her receive the money ; and I helped her to bring it home, and I saw her put it there," said the housekeeper, indicating the place where the widow had deposited it,—and I know that it was there the night before she died, *povera buon' anima!* And when I came to look for it after her death, as it was right and fitting I should look, the money was gone ! And if it was not for doing what is right, why should I tell you at all anything about it ; for you knew nothing, and but for me never would have known nothing ! " said the Signora Sibilla, concluding with—" And now, Signor Carlo, what do you think of that ? "

" I can but suppose that the money has been stolen, signora. You know best who can have had access to it," said Carlo.

"How can I tell? Pretty well anybody in all the town might have got at it that morning that your blessed mother died. She was brought in by one of the neighbours from where she was found lying; and it was some time before I was called, or knew anything about it. There was ever so many people in the house when I got here;—any of the neighbours who chose to come in;—a work I had to clear the house of them!"

"No doubt the money must have been taken during that time," said Carlo.

"One would say so!" answered Sibilla, reflectively; "but think of such a sum as ten thousand dollars, Signor Carlo! Who on earth is there up here who could have taken such a sum as that?"

"Heaven only knows!" said Carlo, wearily and sadly; "who can say how robberies take place? Any way, this money was ill gained; and they say, you know, Signora Sibilla, that ill gains go badly."

"Ill gains!" exclaimed Sibilla, lifting up her hands in deprecatory astonishment; "what do you call ill gains, Signor Carlo? Surely a prize in the lottery is a lawful gain anyway ;—ay, and a blessed gain too, when it comes as it did to that poor saint as is gone, from the blessed Saints themselves!"

" At all events," said Carlo, waiving further discussion on this point, "the thief, whoever he was, had none the more right to put his hand on a dollar of the money."

" *Diamine!* The money was yours, Signor Carlo ;—ten thousand dollars ;—barring what you would think right to compliment me with, as helped your blessed mother in the getting of it ; which can be proved, the more so as it was my own brother who gave seven-and-twenty dollars for the crucifix because I recommended your dear mother to him, and who stood by her in her last moments, and was the only friend she had to look to ;—and had promised me to think of me handsome !" concluded Sibilla, reflecting that any words she chose to put into the mouth of the deceased woman could never be disproved.

" Would she had lived to do so, Signora

Sibilla, and to enjoy her extraordinary good
fortune herself!" said Carlo, uttering one of
those *banalités* people are apt to fall into when
they have nothing better to say.

"Ah! poor dear! would she had! It would
have been a great thing for me!—putting aside
that we loved each other as we did, and had
done for many a long year! But, Signor Carlo,
what do you mean to do about the money?"
said Sibilla, anxiously.

"Do, Signora Sibilla? What can I do?
You tell me the money has flown away as
quickly as it came," said Carlo, with a sigh.

"Flown away! Ten thousand dollars don't
fly away without hands, Signor Carlo!"

"Nor five hundred either!" said Carlo.

"In course not!" said the Signora Sibilla,
rather surprised at the somewhat unpractical
nature of the reply;—"in course not! The
money was stolen. What shall you do about
it, I ask you, Signor Carlo?"

"And I ask you, signora, what can I do?"
repeated Carlo, whose main anxiety at the
moment was that the Signora Sibilla should go

away and leave him in peace to his own
thoughts.

" Well, I am but a poor woman, but I think
I know what ought to be done, and that this
very hour. If I was you, Signor Carlo, I
should go directly to the *giandarmi* here, and
then to the *tribunale* at Pescia. Perhaps, too,
you would like to speak to his Reverence."

" Yes ! of course I must call on his Reverence !
Do you think it would be convenient for me to
go now, Signora Sibilla ? " said Carlo, catching
at a chance of bringing his *tête-à-tête* with his
visitor to an end.

" Yes, surely ! Signor Carlo ; his Reverence
will be very glad to see you," replied the housekeeper. " You won't say anything to his Reverence of what I have told you, Signor Carlo,
about my having helped your mother in getting
her lottery-ticket. He might be angry with me
about it. And you would not get me into
trouble ? "

" Very well, then ! I will go at once. No !
I won't say anything ; never fear ! There will
be no need to speak on the subject," said Carlo ;

and so he and the Signora Sibilla walked up the
street together.

The priest received him with all possible
courtesy, and the usual phrases of condolence
proper for the occasion, judiciously mingled
with a gentle professional hint or two as to the
propriety of "doing something" for the soul of
that excellent Christian whom they had lost.
They were not put so directly as to require an
immediate reply, and Carlo having said what it
was a matter of course to say, and having
thanked the priest for his letter, and for having
allowed his housekeeper to look to the house
after his mother's death, turned as if about to
take his leave, without having said a word on
the subject on which the priest was specially
prepared to hear him speak. The housekeeper
had not judged it to be desirable to say anything to her employer about the loss of the
money. To do so would have involved the
necessity of telling the whole story of the
lottery-ticket, and of her part in the matter.
And this, for many reasons, she was unwilling
to do. She knew, of course, that he must

eventually hear all about it, and must become
aware that she herself had known it previously.
But he need never know how long previously.
The widow might have made the housekeeper
her confidante on the evening before her death.
And she might easily account for not having
told him of the facts during the few hours that
had elapsed since on the score of the shock
occasioned by the widow's sudden death, and
the various matters which she had had to
occupy her in consequence of that event. She
would fain have avoided the necessity of telling
him anything about it. But that was incom-
patible with her hope that the money might
yet be recovered. For she felt that Carlo
would naturally speak openly on the subject.

All these motives the priest calculated on
accurately enough. He did not doubt that
Sibilla would have taken the earliest opportunity
of telling Carlo all about it, having sufficiently
satisfied herself that it absolutely was not in the
house. He was, therefore, greatly surprised,
and almost alarmed, at the young man's being

apparently about to leave him without speaking on the subject.

Carlo, however, had not intended to go without a word respecting the important loss of which Sibilla had told him ; though he did not at all see how it was likely that the priest would be able to assist him.

" There is another matter, *Signor Parroco,* which, perhaps, I ought to mention to you, though I hardly know that I have any right to trouble you with it," said he, already standing up to go.

" If it is aught that troubles you, my young friend, you have every right to trouble me with it. For what else are we ministers of the Gospel placed here ? " said the priest, with a sudden assumption of the unctuous manner which he reserved for certain occasions, and which was quite as different from his ordinary mode of talking as his intoning in church was from his out-of-church utterances.

Carlo merely bowed in return for the bit of hypocrisy. " The Signora Sibilla, your house-keeper," he said, " has been telling me a strange story about a prize of very large amount which, she says, my poor mother won in the lottery a very few days before she died. The money, she tells me, was all in the house, to her knowledge, the .evening previously, and cannot now be found. She considers that it must have been stolen by some one of those who entered the house the morning that my poor mother lay insensible and dying."

The priest paused a minute before replying. Much as he had thought about this expected interview with Carlo on the subject of the missing money, it had, strangely enough, never occurred to him to make up his mind whether he should admit that he had been aware of the widow's good fortune, or should declare that he then heard of the matter for the first time. Bringing his mind to bear on all the circumstances as rapidly as he could, it struck him that it very probably might be known in the town that the widow Caroli had had more than one long interview with him on the day before she died. And it would seem too improbable that she should not then have mentioned what had happened to her, or indeed that her visit to him should not have had special reference to that subject.

So he decided on saying that he was aware of the prize having been won.

" You don't say so ! " said he, starting back, and holding up his hands in well-acted dismay. " Your poor dear mother had communicated to me the great piece of good fortune, which by the blessing of heaven had befallen her, and I had hoped that it would have been the means of making you quite comfortable, Signor Carlo. The sum I understood was a very large one. Good heaven ! And now you tell me that it has been stolen ! "

" I am surprised that your Reverence did not mention anything of this in your letter," said Carlo, simply as the idea rose in his mind that it was odd that the priest had not done so.

" I abstained from doing so, partly because I did not wish to mingle such matters with the awful tidings which it was my painful duty to communicate to you, my young friend ; and partly because I wished to have the pleasure of telling you of your good fortune by word of mouth. But my housekeeper has been beforehand with me! . . . . And now you tell me that the money has been stolen! What did you say was the amount?"

" I did not name it. *La Signora* Sibilla told me that it was ten thousand dollars ;—an immense sum," said Carlo.

" Good gracious ; yes ! I understood that it was a very large sum. I think that *was* the sum your poor mother mentioned. She was very anxious to expend a portion of it in masses for the soul of your good father ! And now . . . . she has need of similar charity herself,— more need, indeed, than he had. For alas, she died without the sacraments of the Church!—not by the fault of any one," the priest hastened to add—" but by the misfortune of her very sudden and unexpected death. Alas! that it should have been so."

" May I ask if you agree with the Signora Sibilla, *Signor Parroco,* in thinking that this money has been stolen from my mother's house ?" asked Carlo, directly.

" Well, it is very difficult to form an opinion.
I have not had time to consider the matter. It
is so shocking! Stolen from the house! It
seems hardly likely! Our people here, as none
know better than yourself, Signor Carlo, are for
the most part honest enough,—*buona gente!*
And such a theft from a house, under such circumstances! I hardly think . . . ."

" Still, *Reverendo Signore,* if the Signora
Sibilla knows that the money was in the house
on the night before my mother died . . . ." said
Carlo.

" It is very singular,—very singular certainly
. . . . and very distressing! But perhaps it is
not necessary to account for the disappearance
of the money by such a supposition. May not
your mother have been afraid to keep such a
sum in the house? May she not have con-
cealed it for greater safety in some place out of
the house?—by burying it in the forest, perhaps. May not her errand out of doors on the
night of her death, been just this?" suggested
the priest.

" It may have been so, certainly," replied

Carlo, thoughtfully ;—" it may have been so, but it is not like my mother. I should be surprised to find that such had been the case. Well, *Signor Parroco*, pardon my having troubled your Reverence with such matters. I will not intrude on you longer. *A rivederla!*"

Carlo walked forth from the priest's house, deeply meditating many things. Turning towards the church he passed round the eastern end of it into the solitary churchyard, and stood for a few minutes at the foot of the grave that had so recently closed over his father. He felt an insuperable reluctance in his present frame of mind to return immediately to the town, probably to fall again into the hands of the Signora Sibilla. So turning his face towards the mountain behind the church, he strolled on in that direction through the forest.

All the town of Uzzano, as has been said, is situated on the south of the church, and a little below it on the slope of the mountain side. But there are a few isolated dwellings higher up among the chestnut wood, not so near as to be visible from the churchyard, but at no great distance up the mountain.

Carlo wandered up the path through the wood, towards these, not with any intention of going thither or elsewhere, but simply seeking solitude, and an hour for indulging his own meditations in freedom from interruption. He wanted to think over the startling news which he had heard from the Signora Sibilla ; and some of the words which had dropped from the priest had set his mind at work uneasily. But his mind, when left free to follow its own course, would still turn only to one and the same direction. He had thrown himself on the turf under the huge hollow trunk of an aged chestnut, the vast upper boughs of which presented as flourishing a world of greenery, as if the patriarch of the forest had been as sound at the core as a comely young tree ;—as is the manner of the fathers of the chestnut grove. He was equally out of sight of the town, and of the dwellings higher up, which have been spoken of; and he lay looking out over the distant lowlands in the direction of Lucca, now bathed in the golden

light of the autumn setting sun. Towards
Lucca he looked! And the hint was sufficient
to put the lottery-ticket and the mysteries connected with it out of his mind, and to send his
musings to the sad subject of his ruined and
lost love.

There was nothing to be thought *out* in this
direction. His thinkings were a mere miserable
impasse, which could lead to nothing, and might
have lasted till the already fading glory of the
sunset had all gone to grey—to leaden colour,—
to deepest indigo,—to the silver witch-light of
the rising moon, had he not been disturbed by
the loud and bitter wailing of a child,—a little
girl of some ten years old,—who came down
the path from the hamlet further up the mountain towards the town. Carlo knew the child,
as soon as she came near enough to be seen,
and called to her to ask what was her trouble.

He soon learned that the same misfortune
had happened to the child as to him. She had
lost her mother! Carlo had known the woman
well, as the inhabitant of one of the little cottage farms up the mountain. He made the

little one sit down on the turf by him, set himself to comfort her, and in doing so learned all
her troubles. Her mother's death was not all,—
was not even the worst! She had died without
the sacraments of the Church! She too! Another touching point of their two cases. The
poor woman had died, he found, but a few hours
before the death of his own mother. And the
child had been sent down the mountain,—the
only messenger from the lone cottage that could
be spared,—to call the priest, but had failed to
find him. And she had been blamed, and father
was very angry with her, and the *Signor Parroco* too. It was very hard! She had done all
she could, but nobody had answered the bell;
—the night-bell, with which every parsonage
house is provided specially for such needs as
that of little Beppina Trilli.

"Are you sure nobody came in answer to the
bell, Beppina? Did you wait?"

"Yes! ever so long I waited. The moon was
shining over the big chestnuts in the churchyard
when I came down the hill, and when I ran
away it was shining over the castle."

"Did you ring more than once?" asked Carlo.

"Yes, Signor Carlo, three times before I ran away."

"Ran away! why did you run away?"

"Nobody would come. I rang three times!" said the child, repeating the excuses she had made often before in replying to the blame cast on her for the failure of her errand.

"But you said you ran away. What made you run away, little one, eh?

Carlo was one of those endowed with the special gift of attracting children and gaining their confidence. Dogs place immediate trust in certain persons, it is difficult to say why. And children do much the same. Carlo was one of these children-charmers. And in answer to his gentle questionings, Beppina, after some hesitation, told him what she had never ventured to tell anybody else.

"Please, Signor Carlo,—but you must not tell anybody,—please—it was a bogy that frightened me."

"Nonsense, little one! there are no bogies!

you were frightened by the shadows in the moonlight.   Poor little Beppina!"

Beppina shook her head.

" Please, Signor Carlo, I know the shadows in the moonlight, and how they move, and change.   I am not frightened at them.   But I *did* see a bogy coming round the end of the church."

" What did the bogy look like, Beppina?"

" It was all white, with black legs! It had no arms! And it was coming quick, quick, straight towards me!"

" And where were you, then, *Beppina mia?*" asked Carlo, looking at the child attentively.

" I was standing close to the door of the *cura*.   I had just rung the bell the third time," said Beppina.

" And then you were frightened and ran away.   Which way did you run, my child?"

I ran round the corner of the *cura*, the other corner, the contrary way to that the bogy was coming.   And I peeped round the corner, and I saw the bogy go into the *cura*, through the door, without opening it, or ringing or anything.

And then I ran away as fast as ever I could, and ran home. And mother died soon after, and never had the sacraments. And father said it was my fault."

" But did you tell your father of the bogy, Beppina ?"

" No, Signor Carlo, I was afraid! I have never told anybody except you. But it is true, indeed, indeed, that I did see him, and I saw him go into the house of the *Signor Parroco.*"

" And when he came as close to you, as the distance from the corner of the house to the door, did he still seem to be dressed all in white, my child ?"

" Yes, Signor Carlo. I saw him quite plain ! He was all white except the legs. He had black legs ! Oh, I was so frightened ! "

Carlo said what he could to comfort the child, and got up from the turf, and walked with her as far as the entrance to the town, where he parted with her to turn his own sauntering steps towards his own house.

At the door of it, trying as ineffectually as little Beppina at the door of the *cura* to make somebody within hear him, he found Moro, the son of old Caterina,—who it may be remembered had done for his mother on the night of the flood, that which Carlo had done for Regina.

CHAPTER VIII.

A POST! POST HASTE!

"WHAT, Moro ! is that you ?" cried Carlo, in great surprise. " What on earth brings you to Uzzano ? You are looking for me, too, as I guess by finding you at this door. There is nobody else to be found in this house now !"

"Nor you neither, Signor Carlo, seemingly. Yes! signor, I was looking for you. I have got a letter for you!"

"A letter for me!" said Carlo, changing colour ;—"from Signora Monaldi, I suppose ?" he said, stretching out his hand for it. "And do you mean that you have come all the way from Lucca to bring a letter to me ?"

"Yes, Signor Carlo ;—because I was ordered so to do. But the letter ain't from the Signora

Monaldi at all. It is from,—anyway, it was
given to me by the Signorina Regina."

Carlo's heart gave such a leap that he felt
as if he was choking. "From the Signorina
Regina!" he said, in a voice as much like his
usual one as he could make it; "where is it,
man? Why don't you give it to me?"

"*Pazienza!* signore. Here it is! I put it
into the inside pocket of my jacket for safety."

"Did the signorina herself give it to you,
Moro mio? and what did she say?

"She told me I was to carry this to Uzzano;
—that I must lose no time, and you must have it
to-night anyway. And I was well paid for the
job! But I didn't stop at Pescia, not a minute
to get a morsel of food, and ...."

"You are starving, of course, *povero mio!*
Come in, and .... or, stay! I will take you to a
trattoria, where you will get something better
than you will in this empty house! Come
along, *pago io.* I stand treat, you know," said
Carlo, remembering the very small means there
were in the house of finding food.

They went together to the *trattoria*, and

Carlo having ordered a good meal for Regina's courier, left him, telling him when he had finished eating to come back to him at his own house. He was thus left at liberty to devour the contents of his letter in peace.

Rushing home, he shut and bolted the stout door behind him as he entered, and bounding up the stairs to the chamber which used to be his own, and which has been described in a former chapter, he sat at the window overlooking the forest, and after kissing the paper all over, broke it open, and read as follows—

"Thanks, *Carlo mio*, for your letter, and for every word in it! Every word! You do me justice—and no more than justice—in feeling sure that I should not for an instant believe any such monstrous calumny as the stupid tale you tell me. I had heard it all already. Our dear friend Signor Meo Morini had the special kindness to come with all speed to me to tell me all about it. Ugh! what a man that is! To think of the stupidity of the creature,—to speak of nothing else! He pretends to be anxious

that I should like him! and that is the way
he takes to make himself agreeable to me! I
think I succeeded in undeceiving him on that
point.

"You won't be angry at my sending a special
messenger after you all the way to Uzzano,
dear Carlo! You will say I might have sent
my letter by the post. But it would not have
reached you before to-morrow morning; perhaps not before the middle of the day. And I
was so anxious that you should have my letter
to-night. For I hope it may help to make you
have a less sad night, *Carlo mio!*—to make us
have a less sad night. For you will not doubt
that my hours pass as unhappily as yours,
while I know that you are away from me and
suffering. It breaks my heart, my own love,
to think that so much trouble should have
come upon you all in a nasty lump altogether.
I know well what it is to lose a mother, though
not to lose her, as has been your case, in absence. For my mother died in my arms. And
I can imagine how such a loss must make such
a heart as yours sore, my Carlo! For such

griefs there is no remedy save that which
God sends in his own time. You were a good
son, and that reflection must be your consolation in your sorrow.

"But with regard to this other bothersome
business, I really think, my Carlo, that you take
it too much to heart. You wrong many people
in saying that they all will believe such an absurdity or to suppose you could be guilty of
such a crime. The widow herself did not believe it, to start with. God bless her ! I shall
always love her for her generous heart. But
observe, signore, I will take upon myself all that
part of your debt of gratitude. *You* need not
love the widow. Do you mark me ? You see
I can laugh, my Carlo !—which I surely could
not if things were as bad as you describe them.

"Then, again, there is my dear father ! He
does not believe you guilty, I can assure you !
He won't hear of it ; and says in reply to all
they tell him, that 'Carlo Caroli is not of
the sort of stuff thieves are made of !' Is not
that a good answer ? Ah ! father has a good
heart ; he has, indeed, my Carlo.

"And now, what will you say when I tell
you that, as far as I can see, this story of the
money that has been stolen from the Signora
Monaldi is likely to turn out the very best thing
that could have happened to us? Now don't
sneer a bitter sneer! All will be found out one of
these days, and it will be proved who stole the
money. I feel sure it will. And in the meantime the calumny has at least done us this good
service. My father has sworn in the most
violent manner, that Meo Morini shall never
marry a daughter of his. And you know that
such was his wish and his determination. You
know how miserable it made me, and you know
that it was the greatest difficulty before us. Now
I must tell you that it was Signor Meo who sent
the *giandarmi* out to Sponda Lunga, making
them think, it seems, that he was sent with a
message to them from the widow. And father
found all that out. And when Signor Meo
came to him telling him all the story against
you, just as if it was the best news in the world,
and showing that he was as glad of it as could
be, and was obliged to confess that it was he

who had run to the *giandarmi* to give them the
information, didn't father go into one of his
passions! And didn't he tell Signor Meo a
piece of his mind! He told him he was nothing but a vile informer, and swore that such
as he should never marry his daughter! I
cannot tell you what a relief and a happiness it
has been to me. And you will understand that
I could not rest till you had heard my good
news. Signor Meo did not come to supper that
night. He was ashamed to show his face. But
Signor Morini tried all he could to come round
father, and soften him down. But it would not
do! Father was out and out disgusted at the
malice of the odious creature, and at the impu-
dent way he took it for granted that other
people were as malicious as he. And then
running to give information to the police in that
way! Why, as father said, a paid spy could do
no more than that. And you may be quite
sure father will not forgive or forget it in a
hurry. And is not this good news, *Carlo mio?*
I don't know when I have heard anything that
has made me so happy; except, by-the-by, some-

thing that was told me one evening after supper
at Ripalta—poor old Ripalta!—one evening
when Signor Meo Morini was there to supper :—
and a certain other person, who I remember
mentioned a wonderful fact to me after supper
in a great hurry, and then ran off without
waiting for an answer. Yes! that, I think,
made me happier still! But it is a very good
thing to be no longer threatened with the ' devoted attachment' of Signor Meo !

"And I have one other thing to tell you,
dear Carlo, which I think you will be glad to
hear, because it seems to me that it will go a
long way towards finding out the thief who stole
Signora Monaldi's money. It seems that the
dollars were sent to the widow by Lawyer
Morini, and that they were all marked in a certain way ; and that the lawyer can swear to the
marks. Other people think that this will help
very much to find out the thief. Another dollar
marked in the same way has been put into the
hands of the police ; and the mark has been
pointed out to them, and they say that this
will help them very much in catching the thief.

So this is another bit of good news, is it not, my poor troubled Carlo? Don't let the trouble fret you, my own love! Trust me, all will come right! All! Yes, all! And that is a great deal, is it not? considering what goes to the making all right for you and me!

"And now I have told you all my good news, I have a good mind to be cross and give you a good scolding. I certainly should, if it were not that I have already written such a monstrous long letter, and that I want to send it off. I have sent for Moro. His mother promised me that he should come directly, and I suppose he will be here presently, in time to start for Pescia by the afternoon train. Never call me 'Signorina Regina' again, sir! or I will call you 'Signor Carlo' to the end of my days; and never believe again that, whether in joy or in sorrow, in good report or in evil report, in prosperity or in adversity, in sickness or in health, I can or ever shall be anything but,

> " Your own ever loving
> "REGINA."

Carlo read the letter straight on from beginning to end.   His emotions, as he read,
were almost too strong to permit him to do so.
But the longing desire and anxiety to possess
himself of what came next was too great to
allow him to pause.   When he came to the end
his bosom swelled and the tears came into his
eyes.   The immense joy that filled his heart to
overflowing was almost too much ;—seemed, in
its intensity, almost to touch the verge of pain.
He got up from his chair, and moved from side
to side of the little chamber, with irregular
step.   Then throwing himself on his knees
at the foot of the bed, he exhaled the
emotions which were almost choking him, in
what he honestly meant to be thanksgiving
to the Author of all mercies and all good ;
but which, in truth, scarcely succeeded in
raising his mental vision to any higher sphere
than that occupied by the earthly saint of his
adoration.

Was she not worthy of every highest,
tenderest, noblest thought a lover's mind could
mint !   And all the tenderness, the delicacy,

the sweetness manifested in the letter he had just read, Carlo was capable of appreciating at its due worth, as few, it may be feared, of those around him, who were his equals in social position, would have been capable. His old friend and master, the recluse Swiss philosopher, whose home had been at Pescia for so many years, would have been proud to see that the culture he had bestowed had produced good fruit. Carlo felt with a delicacy, of which no uncultured mind would have been capable, how much of the frank lovingness of the letter he had just read he owed to his own position,— not of the love of the girl, but of the loving tone of her letter. How dear, how noble was the heart that could thus cast aside all the little coynesses and girlish pride in the necessity of pouring balm into the wounds of the man she loved! How exquisite was the tone in which she spoke of all the circumstances affecting him as of matters in which they both had a common interest!

Then suddenly sprung into his mind an eager desire to pour out all his heart in reply. If

only he could have that minute poured into her ear all that it was in his heart to say! He could but write. And that brought back his mind to Moro. He ought to have come back from the *trattoria* by this time. Carlo deter-
.mined to go and look for him, and ascertain when the messenger thought of starting on his return to Lucca.

He found Moro with his head upon his arms, and his arms upon the table, in the place where he had eaten his supper, and fast asleep.

"I was just thinking what we should do with him, Signor Carlo!" said the landlord; "he don't seem much inclined to move; and it's time for us to be shutting up."

Carlo, not without a good deal of shaking, succeeded in rousing poor Moro from his well-earned sleep; and telling him that he had better come and sleep in his house, asked him when he intended to set out on his journey home. Moro professed himself ready to go at once. But there was no train during the night. The earliest train was one which left Florence at five in the morning, and would pass Pistoia on its way to Lucca at a little after seven. So it was settled that Moro should finish his sleep in "Casa Caroli," and start on his way down the hill at five, or not much after, the next morning.

And then Carlo sat down to write. He felt none of the difficulty in commencing his letter, which had detained him so long the previous night at Sponda Lunga. His pen ran on now as the pen of a ready writer. There is no necessity for copying his letter here. For few readers would have any difficulty in imagining all he said;—even though the all was a great deal. It was a much longer letter than his last; and was in parts, it may be feared, somewhat repetitive. But this was a fault with which his correspondent found no fault.

When the letter was written it was past midnight. Carlo having thus found a vent for the rushing overflow of his emotions, was now somewhat more calm. Still his mind and heart were far too full for it to be possible for him to think of going to bed. There was so much to think of! And all he had thought of as yet had been of Regina and her love!

There was that circumstance of the marks on the money stolen from the widow's house. Surely, if the police could be moved to be sufficiently active, this must sooner or later afford a means of tracing the thief. Five hundred dollar pieces; and all marked, while the thieves were in ignorance of any such fact! It could hardly be but some of these marked dollars would ere long be found! Would it not be well for him to put himself in communication with the heads of the police respecting this matter?

Then the extraordinary facts that the Signora Sibilla had revealed to him! He had hardly yet given a thought to the possibility of recovering this money. It seemed to him almost fabulous that it should ever have existed. Yet the fact of this wonderful prize having been won by his mother had been confirmed by the priest! Ten thousand dollars! Could it be possible that it was on the cards, that he might be—if it could ever be found!—the possessor of such a sum! Carlo was very far from being particularly greedy of money. But he could not prevent it from flashing through his mind that the possession of such a sum would probably, in the farmer's present disposition of mind, remove all difficulty in the way of an union between Regina and himself, ... supposing, he added to himself, with a sigh, his name should have been effectually cleared from all shadow of ill-repute in the matter of the Sponda Lunga robbery.

And then his mind reverted to the tale which little Beppina Trilli had told him. And some of the circumstances of it set him thinking deeply. He had already made careful inquiry among the neighbours, and had ascertained that none of them had seen the widow Caroli leave her house on the evening of the day before her death. He had, on the other hand, been able to find persons who had passed the steps, on which his mother had been found in the morning, at a late hour the preceding evening, and who could speak with certainty to the fact of there having been nobody there then. His

mother must, therefore, have left her house
quite late in the night! It was very strange!
very unlike anything which he could have
supposed her likely to do!—very unaccount-
able! Then the lateness of the hour up to
which he had been able to ascertain that she
was *not* on the steps, brought the time at which
she must, in all probability have gone there
very near the time at which little Beppina had
seen whatever it was that had frightened her!
Could there have been any connection between
the fright of the child and the accident which
had happened to his mother? Had she been
frightened by the same appearance, whatever it
may have been? And had any such fright
been the cause of her fall on the steps, and of
the condition in which she was found there?
It did seem very probable that such might have
been the case! And little Beppina was positive
that she had seen "the bogy" enter the priest's
house! It was possible that all her story was
the mere creation of her excited and alarmed
imagination. But still the child spoke very
calmly, very consistently, and very clearly.

The Signora Sibilla! could she have been the bogy? If she were, and if there were any connection between the bogy and the fate which had befallen his mother, and, again, between this fate and the disappearance of the money, as he could not help suspecting, the house-keeper would assuredly not, in such case, have communicated the story of the lottery ticket to him at all. No! it was clear that Sibilla was innocent of all knowledge of the whereabouts of the missing sum.

The priest himself! Carlo's thought was gradually and inevitably driven in this direc-tion. If it were the fact that the child had seen somebody enter the *cura* in the manner she had described, it could only have been one of the inmates. And the inmates consisted solely of the priest and his housekeeper. There was a lad who did the rougher part of the priest's household service,—but he did not sleep in the house. If, then, anybody really did enter in the depth of the night into the house of the *parroco* in the manner described by the child, it must have been the priest. But for

K 2

what possible purpose could it be supposed that
he was abroad in such a costume as little
Beppina had described. The bogy had black
legs. Yes! that would tally well enough. But
the rest of the figure was all white! Carlo
pondered deeply and long. And the more he
pondered, the more strong became his persuasion that there was, at least, a great
probability that the priest knew more than he
chose to tell of the circumstances that had led
to his mother's fall on the steps of the churchyard, and consequent death; and further, that
it was far from impossible that these facts
might be connected with the disappearance of
the money.

The end at which his meditations arrived
was, that he would take the Signora Sibilla's
advice as to consulting the police authorities at
Pescia on the subject. He determined that
he would not make any application to the
giandarmi stationed at Uzzano. They would
probably have taken some immediate step,
which might only have the effect of putting the
parties concerned on their guard. He thought

it best to lay the whole case before a more
competent and intelligent authority. And in
the case he meant to include the statements of
little Beppina Trilli.

There was one other matter that occurred to
him in connection with this strange story of the
purchase of the lottery-ticket by his mother.
This purchase had taken place just after the
time when he must, according to the theory of
those who believed him guilty, have stolen the
five hundred dollars from the widow Monaldi.
Now it was sufficiently notorious that his
mother had been left in circumstances approaching to destitution. Yet she was found just at
that time expending the serious sum of ten
dollars on a lottery-ticket. He felt that the
evidence of the Signora Sibilla as to the source
from which this money had been provided was
most important to him. And he determined,
therefore, in telling the story he had to tell to
the Commissary of Police at Pescia, to point
out this circumstance, and as a necessary consequence to relate the story of the loss of, the
money at Sponda Lunga.

It was past one o'clock by the time he had arrived at this decision. But there was still time for two or three hours' sleep before he had to rouse Moro, and start him on his homeward journey.

When he did so, he told him that he would himself accompany him as far as Pescia. And at five o'clock, when scarcely a soul was stirring in Uzzano, Carlo locked the door of his house behind him, and set off with Moro on his walk down the mountain.

BOOK V.

CAUGHT IN HIS OWN TRAP

CHAPTER I.

CARLO said good-bye to Moro when they reached Pescia, bidding him make all speed with his letter to Regina, and telling him no more of his present errand than that he had some business to attend to in the town. And, having seen him off by the train they had intended to catch, Carlo sought the office of the Commissary of Police.

His interview with that functionary was a long one. He had a long story, or rather two long stories to tell, and his auditor evidently seemed to think many of the special circumstances to which Carlo called his attention highly important. When he came to the revelations of Beppina Trilli, telling the Commissary at the same time that he knew the child, and

felt convinced that she was in any case saying
what she believed to be true ; the Commissary,
telling him to stop a minute, took a small
volume from a locked drawer, turned over the
leaves rapidly, till he came apparently to the
passage he was looking for, and then, nodding
his head with an air that seemed to say,
" Ay ! ay ! I thought so ! " returned the
volume to its place, and carefully relocked the
drawer.

" I am inclined to think, Signor Caroli," he
said, looking up after a pause given to thought,
" that your suspicions have hit the right nail on
the head.   I think that the Reverend Pasquale
Mommi knows more about this matter than we
do ; and that, if we set about it judiciously, he
might perhaps be persuaded to give us some
valuable information.   The woman, who told
you of the purchase of the lottery-ticket, you
say, is his housekeeper ? "

" Yes !   Sibilla Gralli, she is the priest's
housekeeper."

" Her evidence, of course, would be forth-
coming.   In telling you of the sale of the

crucifix, did she say to whom it had been sold ? " asked the Commissary.

" Yes, she said it had been sold to her brother, Signor Stefano Gralli, a goldsmith and jeweller on the Ponte Vecchio at Florence. She boasted that it was due to her recommendation that so large a sum as twenty-seven dollars had been received for it," answered Carlo.

" Signor Stefano Gralli ! " repeated the Commissary, thoughtfully. " Why, let me see, surely that is the name . . . . " he said, putting his hand on a packet of papers lying on his desk as he spoke ; " . . . . yes, Stefano Gralli, jeweller, on the bridge at Florence ! very good ! The crucifix was sold to Signor Stefano Gralli, who gave seven-and-twenty dollars for it, very good ! " said the Commissary, making a note of the facts.

" Now, Signor Caroli," he continued, " this is what I shall do in the first place. I shall take a walk up the hill to Uzzano, and I shall take the liberty of searching the priest's house pretty thoroughly. I am not sure that the facts we are in possession of would justify me in taking such a course with a parish priest in general, but," tapping the drawer which contained the little book he had consulted with his finger, " . . . . in the case of the Reverend Pasquale Mommi, that is the course I shall take."

" Would you wish me to go up to Uzzano with you?" asked Carlo.

" Well, no! I think you had better not. I shall not think it necessary in the first instance to tell the *parroco* what is the object of my perquisition. He will probably be able to guess it. I shall search the house as quietly as possible, without making any scandal. And if I find nothing, there will be no harm done, and the reverend gentleman will have only his own past history to thank for the inconvenience I shall put him to. No! I think you had better stay away from Uzzano just for a little while, now you are away."

Carlo, when he had decided on accompanying Moro down the mountain, had fully intended to return to Uzzano as soon as he should have had his interview with the Police Commissary; but, on hearing the above advice, his heart jumped at

the idea of at once returning to Lucca.   It was
not that he had at the moment any idea that he
should have an opportunity of seeing Regina, but
it seemed as if it would be a comfort to him to
be in her near neighbourhood.   He had, too, a
nervous sort of anxiety to be on the spot where
the loss of the widow Monaldi's money was, he
hoped, being judicially inquired into ;—where,
at least, it was the subject of gossip and specula-
tion. He was anxious to know what people were
saying about it ;—whether any circumstance
had come to light ;—whether any prospect of
discovering the mystery seemed to be opening
itself.   He determined, therefore, to go by the
next train, which would pass at about eleven, to
Lucca.

Meantime his absence from Uzzano had been
observed, and had given rise to some little surprise.   The Signora Sibilla, as early as her
duties in the priest's household would permit of
her doing so, had been to the house of Carlo,
anxious to ascertain what he meant to do in the
matter of the lost money.   She had been able
to obtain no answer to her knocking ; and, on

inquiry, heard from one of the neighbours that
he had been seen leaving the village in company
with the messenger who had come from Lucca
the day before. Sibilla had but little doubt
that he had taken her advice, and had gone
down to see the Commissary of Police. And,
on her return to the priest's house, when he
asked whether Signor Caroli had been able to
hear anything about the missing ten thousand
dollars, she had said that he was gone to
Pescia to give information to the police.

It was about three o'clock in the afternoon of
the same day that the Reverend Pasquale
Mommi was taking his *siesta* after his mid-day
dinner. The Signora Sibilla was sitting at the
window of the room in which the priest was
sleeping with her knitting in her hand. The
room was perfectly still save for the regular snor-
ing of the reverend sleeper. The housekeeper
was as still as a mouse save the occasional
slight click of the knitting needles which she
plied with nimble fingers, while her eyes were
looking out of the window. She was thinking,
however, that it was time to wake his Rever-

ence, for his *siesta* was being prolonged somewhat more than usual.

All of a sudden she did so effectually in a
manner she had not contemplated.

" *Benedicite !* " she exclaimed aloud, jumping
up from her seat as she spoke, and placing herself close to the side of the window, in such a
manner as to command a view from it without
being herself very visible to persons without.
" *Benedicite !* what's the matter now ?   What
can they be a coming here for ? "

" Who are coming here ?   What is it ?   I
wish, Sibilla, you would not make me jump so !
It is very hard one can't be let to have one's
natural rest ! " grumbled the priest, rubbing his
eyes.

" Why, there are a couple of *giandarmi* and
two in plain clothes with them a coming here !
What can they want here, I wonder ?   Yes,
they are coming here, sure enough ! " she
added, and in the same instant the bell at the
door of the *cura* was rung sharply.

" *Giandarmi !* coming here ! " said the priest,
with some signs of disturbance in his manner,

which his housekeeper, engaged in looking
out of window, did not notice. "What can
they want here? Stop, Sibilla! stop a minute
before you open the door! I won't see them! it
is very disagreeable. You will tell them that I
am out ;—gone my rounds through the parish.
I will go into my own room ; and then, if they
have anything to say, you may bring them in
here."

The bell was rung for the second time as the
priest finished speaking, and he and his housekeeper hurried downstairs together, she to open
the door, and he to slip into his own bedroom,
which was on the ground-floor at the back of
the house.

The person in plain clothes who accompanied
the "*giandarmi*," and who was no other than
the Commissary to whom Carlo had spoken at
Pescia, desired to speak to the Reverend Pasquale Mommi. Sibilla said that he was not at
home, being somewhere among the people in
the town, but that the gentlemen could walk in
if they had any business that she could answer
them about.

The gentlemen did walk in, and the *giandarmi* with them.   But the latter advanced no further than the hall, stationing themselves close to the door.   The Commissary and the other officer with him suffered themselves to be led by the Signora Sibilla into the sitting-room upstairs.

" The Signor *Parroco* is not in the house, you say, signora ? " began the Commissary.

" No, signore ! he is out among the people somewhere in the town.   It is a large parish, signore," said Sibilla.

" Well, perhaps he may come in before we go.   For the fact is, signora, we have a little bit of business to do here which may take us some little time.   I am sorry that we shall be obliged perhaps to give you some trouble."

" What . . . . what is it you wish then, signore ? " asked the Signora Sibilla, with a little misgiving.

" Well, the fact is, we shall be obliged to search the house.   It does not follow, you know, signora, that we have anything to say against anybody here.   Not at all!   May be you know, we have heard that somebody has

put gunpowder in the cellars, and means to
blow you all up, and we are come to take care
of your safety!" said the Commissary, with a
smile as cheerful as it was within the bounds of
possibility that the facial muscles of a Commissary of Police should produce.

"*Jesu Maria!*" exclaimed the Signora Sibilla,
who did not seem to take the *badinage* of the
officer at all in the cheerful manner in which it
had been offered.

"Don't be alarmed, signora! We shall make
it all right. Is this the reverend gentleman's
usual sitting-room? Yes! And this bureau?"
pointing to a large old-fashioned piece of furni-
ture as he spoke. "Shall we begin with this?
Would you mind lending us the keys for a
minute?"

"His Reverence has the key of that!" said
Sibilla.

"What a pity he is out," said the officer;
"we shall be obliged to open it somehow."

"Perhaps, signore, I could get the key! His
Reverence the *parroco* very often leaves his keys
in his own room," said Sibilla, with that ready

facility for finding a pretext at which the southron is rarely at fault.

"By all means see if you can find them, signora. They may save us a great deal of trouble. Don't mind about leaving us for a minute or so. We will amuse ourselves with looking round the rest of the apartment!"

Signora Sibilla waited for no second permission to step down stairs to the room in which the priest had taken refuge.

"It is no manner of use hiding here, your Reverence, for they are come to search the house, and they will be here before long! Whatever is it they want?" said the house-keeper, looking much scared.

"Search the house!" cried the priest, turning very pale and then red. "On what pretence, I should like to know? Search my house, indeed! Do they expect to find English Bibles hidden here, I wonder! I won't stay here to be insulted in this way! I shall go out!" and the reverend gentleman turned to the door as he spoke.

"Signor Parroco!" said Sibilla, in an earnest

whisper, laying her hand on his arm. "They have left two *giandarmi* at the door! Perhaps you had better not try to go out!"

"Very well! very well! we shall see what the bishop will say to this! We shall see! But I won't speak with these men! I shall stay here! There;—you may take the keys."

The housekeeper did so, and returned to the room in which she had left the officers. They had evidently been engaged in making a minute search in every part of it. And now they proceeded to search the locked bureau. But there was nothing to be found there tending in any way to throw any light on the matter in hand. They proceeded, accompanied by the housekeeper, to examine carefully every part of the house, room by room, and closet by closet, causing every locked door to be opened for them. All that the faithful Sibilla could do was to manage so that they came last to the room in which the priest had taken refuge. At last they entered that ;—but the priest was not there. The two *giandarmi* were still at the door ; and it was therefore clear that he had not left

the house by that exit.   And the housekeeper
was not aware that there existed any other.

She was not, however, very much surprised at
not finding the priest in his room.   For she *was*
aware that there existed a secret stair of communication between it and the cellars below the
house.   Such constructions are by no means un-
frequent in old Italian houses.   The *cura* was
built on the rock, which had been selected many
hundreds of years ago for the site of the church ;
and large dry cellars, hollowed out of it, existed
under every part of the building.   The Signora
Sibilla doubted not that her reverend master
had retreated by this means of communication
to the cellars.   And she looked forward with
some dread to the awkward moment when he
should be found in so strange a retreat by the
officers.   For she had little or no hope that
the cellars would escape their vigilance.   Even
if they failed to discover the door leading to
the staircase, descending from the priest's room,
which, judging from the way they had examined
every other part of the house, seemed little
likely, they would not fail to observe the principal

approach to the cellars, which was by a door near the foot of the stairs.

The priest's room was scrupulously searched, even to the contents of the mattresses and palliasse of the bed. The latter article of domestic use is more readily turned to the purpose of a hiding place,—and also can be more readily examined,—in Italy than in any other countries.   For it almost always consists of a huge bag filled with the long rustling dry leaves of the maize,—*gran turco*, as it is called in Tuscany ;—and is furnished with openings intended to admit the thrusting in of a hand and arm for the moving and re-arrangement of the leaves.

Nothing, however, was found in the palliasse ; —nothing in any part of the priest's room, save the door opening on the stairs of communication with the cellar.

" Where does this lead to ? " asked the Commissary, opening it, and looking down the dark narrow staircase, constructed in the thickness of one of the foundation walls of the ancient house.

" That, Signor Commissario ! " said Sibilla, who had by this time learned the proper style and title of her visitor, "that only leads to the cellars.   They are quite dark!"

"We must ask of your politeness to provide us with a light then, I am afraid, signora.   For we must not do our work so slovenly as to leave the cellars unvisited.   I dare say his Reverence has a few flasks stowed away there, such as do not see the light every day."

Sibilla proceeded to get a lamp,—one of the old lamps of Etruscan pattern, of beautifully polished and shining brass, on a tall slender stem, two feet high, or nearly so, so universally used in Tuscany.   The lamp itself, which holds the oil, is furnished with three or sometimes four *becs* or burners, and with snuffers, scissors, and a long pin for touching the wick, all of brass, which hang from the stem by little brazen chains. Such a lamp is intended to be carried not by the foot, or by the stem, but by a handle at the upper extremity of the stem, so that the whole machine hangs from the hand, instead of rising from it, in carrying it.

Sibilla brought such a lamp with one of its three *becs*, or burners, lighted.   But the Com-

missary, quietly taking a match from his pocket,
proceeded to light both the others before descending the dark stair.   Then, accompanied
by his follower, and holding the light on high,
he went down, and found himself in what was
evidently a considerable range of cellarage.
The Signora Sibilla did not think it necessary
to follow him down the stairs, preferring probably to be absent when the moment should
arrive at which her master should be discovered in his hiding place.   It was indeed
possible for him to ascend from the cellars by
the stair which formed the main approach to
them ;—but not possible for him so to escape,
because of the two men stationed at the door.

The officers, however, saw no signs of the
presence of the priest.   They had no reason
for expecting to find him, for there was nothing
improbable in the fact stated by the housekeeper, that he was not in the house.   But
neither did the seekers find any indication of
the possible presence of that which they sought.
There was a pile of wood for burning in one
corner ; and they took the trouble of turning

it all over ;—without result. There was a heap of empty flasks in another corner, and a range of full ones standing on some boards in a third. Some of the chambers were absolutely empty. All of them seemed to open into each other, communicating by open arches, in which there were no doors. The officers, therefore, ranged without difficulty through every part of the foundation of the house,—but found nothing ;— neither the priest, nor any signs of what they were in search of.

Returning, therefore, by the way they had come, and beginning to think that their perquisition would lead to nothing, they came back to the chamber they had first entered, immediately under the priest's bedroom. And there, as they turned their faces towards the stair by which they had ascended, the Commissary's eye lighted on a very small, round-arched door, placed so as to be almost hidden behind the bottom steps of the stair. The room above was in the corner of the house nearest to the church, and the little nearly-hidden door in question gave access to a passage communicating with the vaults under the church, and doubtless intended by the builders to afford the priest a means of passing from his own residence to the church without quitting the shelter of a roof. The passage, however, had been long disused, and was closed at what had formerly been the opening into the vaults.

Had it been otherwise, the Reverend Pasquale Mommi might have still baffled his pursuers;—at least as far as his purpose of avoiding personal communication with them went. As it was, he might probably have succeeded in this object, had it pleased him. But things fell out in such sort that he preferred to abandon that purpose.

Immediately on entering the narrow passage which has been described, there was a little door in the outside wall of it. It was not above two feet square and was readily opened. It merely gave access to a small well, opening on the shaft of it, a foot or two below the closed upper end of it. The builders of the house had struck a small spring of clear water in the rock, and had utilised it by constructing this little well. The Commissary explored it by means

of the lamp.   There were only a few inches of
clear water at the bottom of it,—not above five
or six feet below the little door of access.   The
Commissary was holding the lamp down as far
as his arm would reach, with his head and
shoulders leaning through the little doorway,
while his follower behind him was peering over
his shoulders into the lighted-up recess of the
shaft of the well, when suddenly, close to them,
a loud and angry voice demanded " What they
were doing there?"   And coming forth out of
the darkness of the passage, the priest himself
stepped within the little circle of light thrown
on the paved floor by the lamp.

"I am a Commissary of Police, your Reverence," replied the officer, "and information
which has reached me has made it my duty to
search this house.   I am very sorry to have
put you or the signora, your housekeeper, to
any inconvenience.   And I should not have
proceeded to search the rooms or these cellars
except in your presence, but that I was assured
that you were not in the house."

"I have just returned to it!" said the priest,

" and came here to look out a flask of wine for supper. If you will do me the honour to taste a glass, I think you will admit that it was worth the trouble. If you have any business to speak to me on, we had better go upstairs. You seem to have finished your perquisition here." And so saying, the priest made a step towards the little door which led to the cellar in which was the stair, in such sort as to make it necessary for the officers to move in that direction also, or absolutely to bar his progress.

" Yes, your Reverence!" said the Commissary, " I think we have completed our search ; and I am bound to say we have found nothing of any kind to justify it. If you will permit me, I will, as you say, speak with your Reverence a few words upstairs."

He was about to step out of the narrow passage, so as to allow the priest to follow him to the foot of the stairs, when his follower, who had been, as was said, peering into the upper part of the shaft of the little well, while his superior was holding the lamp in the depth below, said—

" *Momento, Signor Commissario ; scusi !* Just
give me the lamp for a moment."

He was standing furthest in the passage from
the door of it ; and the Commissary, pausing
in his way out, handed the man the lamp.

" I fancied," said he, holding the lamp again
into the well, " that I saw something overhead
in the top of the shaft, when you were holding
the light down into the well."

" *Santa Madonna !* What should there be
in the well ?" cried the priest. "Let us get upstairs. We shall all catch our death of cold here."

" One minute, *Signor Parroco*," said the subordinate officer, who had now thrust his head
and shoulders into the shaft of the well in such
sort as to be half-sitting on the sill of the little
square doorway that gave access to it. " Signor
Commissario, I think we've got the article we
are looking for. Here is something in a sack
hanging on to a hook that seems to have served
at one time for a chain to let a bucket down
into the well ;—something precious heavy !"

" Bring it out, Cecco, whatever it is !" said
the Commissary.

"*I* don't know what there may be there, I am sure !" said the priest, in a voice that betrayed his agitation. " Please to observe, Signor Commissario, that I have no knowledge whatever of anything that may be found hidden in these cellars. But, at the same time, I claim that if anything of any value *should* be found,— hidden perhaps by some of my predecessors,—I have the right to appropriate it to my own use. Please to take note of that ! "

" Very good, *Signor Parroco !* I will take note of your protest, and of the claim you set up. Well, Cecco ! What is it ?"

" It is heavy enough to be anything !" said the officer, extricating himself with some difficulty from the small aperture into which he had thrust himself, laden as he was with the lamp and the heavy canvas bag he had taken off the hook at the top of the shaft.

" Now then ! Bring it upstairs ! *Signor Parroco*, if you will follow me, excusing me for going first, we will have a look at our find by daylight."

" Go on, Signor Commissario, I pray you.

Senza complimenti!   I am curious to see what it is you have got there!   Who knows how long it may have been there!" said the priest, following the officer up the secret stair, while the subordinate brought up the rear, carrying the heavy sack.

"Now then," said the Commissary, as soon as they had all three arrived in the priest's chamber; "here, Cecco, put the bag on this table.   *Per Bacco!* there is an ass's load!" he added, putting his hand to the sack.

"Ass's load, *davvero!*" answered Cecco. "But it was the ass who ran down the game, Signor Commissario!"

"Very true, Cecco *mio*, very true!" said the Commissary, untying the sack; while the priest stood by, affecting the greatest curiosity to see what the contents of it might be.   "Hard cash, and no mistake!" continued he, taking a long *rouleau* from the sack.   "Gold, too, *per Bacco!*" he went on, as he unrolled it.   "*Rusponi! Rusponi di zecca!* and what a quantity.   We must count them, *Cecco mio!*   And, *Signor Parroco*, you will have the kindness to observe that they are counted correctly. We shall give you a receipt in due order for them ! "

" Do you mean to say that you are going to carry that gold away with you ? " said the priest, doggedly.

" I am afraid we shall be obliged to do so, *Signor Parroco !* Duty ! duty won't be said 'no' to ! *You* know what duty is, *Signor Parroco !* . . . . One hundred ! Cecco, you count 'em again and chalk down the hundreds . . . . two hundred ! . . . . "

And so on till the whole amount of poor Barbara Caroli's prize was counted out.

" Ten thousand crowns in *rusponi !* Now, Cecco, make up the *rouleau* again ! pop 'em back again into the bag, and tie it up. Ten thousand crowns, your Reverence ! that will be right, won't it ? Now, if you will oblige me with a pen and ink, I will write a receipt for this money, stating that it has been removed from this house by my authority, and that I make myself responsible for the same, undertaking to give account of it, and of my own act in removing it, in due time and place. Then, if you *could* accommodate us with a bit of sealing wax I will seal up the bag, and we shall have all in good order."

The Commissary was evidently in high good humour at the result of his perquisition. The priest was in a very different mood.

"Please to observe, *Signor Commissario*," he said, doggedly, "that I declare, in the first place, that I know nothing whatever of this money; and in the second place, that I protest in the strongest manner against the removal of it. I yield to superior force."

"Of course! of course! *Signor Parroco! A chi lo dite!* Of course you yield to force .... the force of the law! That is understood."

"It is an abuse of power. It is an oppression of the Church;—the money belongs to the Church,—to this benefice! In all probability it was the gift of some pious Christian for devout uses! I protest against this robbery of the Church. We shall see what the bishop of the diocese says to it ; .... and the Nuncio. It will be a matter for Rome!"

"Very likely, *Signor Parroco!* very like it

may! I am but Commissary of Police for the city and district of Pescia! If I should be called to Rome to answer why I seize this money, it would suit my book uncommonly. I never did see Rome! We need not detain your Reverence any longer! See, here is the receipt in due order!"

"I decline to take the paper," said the priest, sullenly.

"Well, it is always a pleasure to us to find something in which we can let people do as they please! We are so often obliged to make 'em do what they don't please! Here's a case in point! I am delighted to tell your Reverence that you may do just as you like about taking the receipt! I put it there on the table! You will do what you please with it. Come, Cecco, shoulder your load! *Reverenza, leveremo l'incommodo! A rivederla!*"

"*Si, Signor Commissario! a rivederla!* You do not suppose that this matter will end here!" growled the priest.

"Surely not! surely not! *diamine! Addio, Signor Parroco!*"

And so the officers bowed themselves out, and being rejoined by the two *giandarmi* they had left in the hall, proceeded down the mountain with their prize, changing the burthen from shoulder to shoulder of the party from time to time. They had said, it will be observed, no word to the priest whose house they had searched, and from whose keeping they were carrying off this large sum of money, about the cause of suspicion against him or their motives for acting as they were doing. Such a mode of procedure may appear strange to English notions, but it was quite according to rule in the place and time in question.

" So, here's the poor old woman's prize in the lottery ! " said the Commissary to his subordinate, as they walked down the mountain side to Pescia. " It cost the poor old soul dear, didn't it ? It'll be a pretty windfall for that young fellow ! I'm glad to have got it out of that old scamp's hands ;—that I am ! "

" But do you know how it got into his hands, Signor Commissario ? " said Cecco.

" I think I understand all about it, *Cecco*

mio !" replied his superior ; " . . . . only a
guess, but I'd lay a largish bet it is a good one.
Look here, the old woman wins a prize in the
lottery ; . . . . just as if those *rusponi* could be
anything else than money paid by the lottery
office ! Stupid old fool, with his talk about his
' predecessors ' and ' devout uses ! ' As if such
chaff as that could take *us* in ! Well, as I was
saying, the old woman wins her prize ; goes, as
they all do, to tell the priest all about it. He
turns it over in his mind how he can lay his
hand on the money;—trumps up some story to
make the poor old soul come out with her cash
in the middle of the night ;—then dresses himself
up as a ghost ;—frightens the life out of her, and
then nabs the cash. And if it had not been for
the queer chance of a child being out at that
hour, and being also frightened by a sight of
the ghost, he would have been safe enough, and
devil a bit would the money ever have been
heard of any more ! "

" *Mamma mia !*" cried Cecco, using an expression very common in the mouths of Tuscans
when intending to express surprise. " Well !

they may say what they will ; but it does seem as if there was a sort of Providence in these things ! "

" To be sure there is, *Cecco mio !* " said the Commissary, slapping his follower on the shoulder ; "and some people call the Providence, ' *Il Commissario di Polizia !* ' "

" And, what will be the upshot of this reverend gentleman's pretty game ? " asked Cecco.

" Well, the young fellow, the old widow's son, will get the money of course, for one thing ! I shall make it a run to Florence ! It is an important case, and there will be other inquiries to make, likely enough ! I shall carry the money to Florence by the evening train to-night."

CHAPTER II.

CARLO, during his journey to Lucca, which he was performing while the police Commissary was making his perquisition in the priest's house at Uzzano, had no little difficulty in making up his mind what he would do as soon as he got thither. What he would have liked to do,— what he was intensely longing to do, was to go straight to Lawyer Morini's house, and ask to see Regina. But the consideration of the position in which he still stood, as one charged with an infamous crime, and believed by many persons to be guilty of it, restrained him. It was true,—and the consideration presented itself again and again to his mind,—that it did not become him to behave as if conscious of having done wrong;—that he ought not to allow himself to be driven, by baseless calumny, into hiding his head!—that he had no reason to be ashamed of himself; and that it was mere moral cowardice to bear himself as if he were ashamed of himself. And he admitted the truth of all such considerations as regarded his bearing towards any other person in the world than Regina. Would it not be taking an ungenerous advantage of her generous conviction of his uprightness and innocence? Might it not be injurious to her in the eyes of those who had no such conviction? Would it not be better to wait till he could, as he began to hope might ere long be the case, present himself before her with his name cleared from every cloud of suspicion? He could hardly go to visit her at the house of the lawyer, even putting out of the question the cloud over him, without an implied assumption in the eyes of the world, of there being something more between them than there was between the Signorina Bartoli and any other of the young men of her acquaintance. Regina accorded him the full right to assume this. But would it be generous of him to take advantage of her having done so just at the present moment? Think of the matter as he would, he could not persuade himself that it would be so.

No! he must abstain! The delight, the infinite joy of hearing her say, with her own sweet words, that she scouted the idea of the man she had loved proving himself to be base and worthless,—of listening to her eager hopefulness as to his complete exoneration,—this must not be his yet! not yet!

But he would show himself in Lucca! he would not sneak off to the privacy of Sponda Lunga, as if he were afraid to meet the eyes of the men who knew him. He would have liked to speak with Lawyer Morini about the marking of those dollars. But he took it for granted that Meo's father would be among those who considered him to be guilty; and he shrunk from the cold, ironical politeness with which the lawyer would, so supposing, "decline to give him information which might be inconsistent with the ends of justice."

Suddenly it occurred to him, that if the con-

siderations referred to above made it improper
for him to ask to see Regina, there were no
reasons against his paying a visit to her father.
Indeed, the kind and friendly view of the
matter which, as he learned from Regina's
letter, the farmer had adopted, made it almost
a duty of gratitude for him to see and thank
Signor Giovanni. He was a shrewd, experienced, and practical man, too, who might be able
to give him some useful word of advice. He
would tell him, too, the story of the lottery ticket.
Perhaps at the bottom of his heart there lay,
unconsciously, a half-formed idea that to the
farmer's mind it might seem less utterly absurd
and out of the question to contemplate as a
son-in-law a man who had been very near
having ten thousand crowns; who, it was still
on the cards, might yet have them !

In short, before he had reached the Lucca
station he had made up his mind that on
arriving, he would walk into the city and call
on Farmer Bartoli.

And it was not till after he had pulled the bell
at the lawyer's door that two difficulties rushed

into his mind. The first was as to the place in which he could expect to see the farmer ;—if downstairs, in the lawyer's studio, the lawyer would probably be there ; if upstairs, there would, doubtless, be some other members of the family present ;—possibly Regina herself. Carlo did not at all like the idea of having his first meeting with his love, after all that had happened, under such circumstances. And he hastily determined that he would ask if the farmer were downstairs, in the *studio* ;—and if he were not, to tell the servant that he would call again. The second difficulty was this !— that if he at once said to the farmer, as he had had it on his lips to say, " I hear that you at least, Signor Giovanni, do not believe me to have been guilty of this crime ! " it would amount to confessing that Regina had written to him. For he could have heard it from no one else. And he had no means of knowing whether Regina had or had not written to him with her father's knowledge.

He had not decided how to meet this second difficulty, when the door was opened ; and he

was told that Signor Bartoli was in the *studio*.
In the next instant Carlo found himself in the
room with the farmer and the lawyer; and
the second of his two difficulties vanished of
itself.

"What, Signor Caroli! Glad to see you, lad!"
said the farmer, coming forward towards him.
"Glad to see you, and to have an opportunity of
telling you that I, for one, never believed a word
of all this story about the widow's money!
Don't tell me! I don't mean that the money
was not stolen, you know! But you were not
the man that stole it! I know better than
that. For all these city folks are so sharp,"—
and the farmer nodded towards the lawyer as
he spoke,—"I often think that we country folk,
for knowing what a man is made of when we
see him, are worth a dozen of them!"

"Your servant, Signor Caroli," said the
lawyer, somewhat drily. "You will admit,
Signor Giovanni, that I have never maintained
that there was a case for a conviction against
Signor Caroli. But it is impossible to deny
that the circumstances are ugly."

"Very ugly, Signor Morini. The more am I beholden to those who have confidence enough in my character to believe in my innocence. Believe me, Signor Giovanni, I shall never forget *your* good opinion of me!—never, to my dying day!" said he, speaking with much emotion. "As to the case, Signor Morini," he went on in a very different tone, turning to the lawyer, "I have been very glad to hear that, as it happens, you are able to state that the dollars which you paid to the Signora Monaldi were all marked, and that you would be able to identify them. It is to be hoped that this may lead to the detection of the thief."

"It is to be hoped so, signore!" answered Morini, still speaking very drily.

"I had occasion, Signor Giovanni," said Carlo, markedly addressing himself to the farmer, "to see the Commissary of Police at Pescia; and he was of opinion that the fact of the money being marked would certainly be of great use."

"What made you go to the Commissary of Police in Pescia about it?" asked the farmer.

"Did you hear anything about it, Signor Carlo, while you were away?"

"No, Signor Giovanni; and it was not about that that I went to the police-office at Pescia. But being there, and speaking to the Commissary, I thought it as well to tell him about it."

"But what was it took you there, then, *figliuolo mio?*" asked the farmer.

"Why, oddly enough," replied Carlo, with rather a pale smile, "while I am accused of stealing other people's money here at Lucca, it would seem as if some thief has been robbing me at Uzzano! And I had to go to the Commissary about that, Signor Giovanni."

"Ah! more likely that than t'other way, I'll answer for it! How was that, then?" asked the farmer.

"Well, it is a long story, and rather a strange one, signor. But to make it short, the fact is that my poor mother, just before her death, bought a ticket in the lottery. The ticket came up a prize. The sum was a large one; and it seems to have been stolen out of the old house at home there, while my poor mother lay dead or dying, and there was no one to look to anything, or prevent anybody from coming into the house who chose. The housekeeper of our *parroco*, who was a friend of my mother's, told me all about it, when I got to Uzzano. I had heard nothing about any lottery ticket."

"And the sum, you say, was a large one?" asked the farmer.

"Yes, indeed, Signor Giovanni, a very large one. Ten thousand dollars! *Niente di meno!*" said Carlo.

"Ten thousand dollars!" exclaimed both the farmer and the lawyer at the same instant. "Ten thousand dollars!"

"Are you sure of the amount, Signor Carlo?" asked the lawyer.

"I can only be sure of what the Signora Sibilla Gralli, the priest's housekeeper, told me," said Carlo. "She said that my mother paid ten dollars for a ticket, on a *terno*; that the *terno* came up; and that she went with my mother to Florence, where the ticket was bought, and saw her receive the money, and helped her to carry it home. She said that she knows that the money was in my mother's house, the evening before she died."

"*Santa Madonna!* Ten thousand crowns!" reiterated the farmer, nearly stunned by the vastness of the sum.

"It is sure enough that that is much about what a *terno* on ten dollars would come to," said the lawyer.

"*Misericordia!* and all that money stolen!" ejaculated the farmer, holding up hands and eyes to heaven, or at least to the rafters of Signor Morini's studio, in dismay.

"Was there any circumstance to point suspicion in any special direction?" asked the lawyer with keen professional interest, and a consciousness of a suddenly increased amount of respect for a man who had so nearly been the owner of ten thousand dollars. "I need not say that if, as is probable, you should require any professional assistance in connection with this matter, we shall be most happy . . . ."

"Thank you, Signor Morini, I am afraid I

hardly see my way yet to any position in which it would be necessary for me to employ a lawyer," said Carlo, rather distantly.

" And as for this other matter, my testimony with respect to the marks on the widow Monaldi's money is ready at any moment. I hope, —indeed I have little doubt, that it may be the means of clearing up that affair satisfactorily ! " said the lawyer, whose views and opinions upon the subject had become suddenly and seriously modified by the startling intelligence he had just heard. How could it be supposed that a man from whom ten thousand dollars had been stolen,—and above all a man who might still possibly recover them,—could be suspected of being guilty of stealing himself?

" Nothing to lead to any clue to what has become of the money ? " asked the farmer, pondering deeply, with his hands deep in his large pockets.

Carlo answered only with his eyes ; but they said plainly enough that he could say more, if he were not restrained by the presence of the lawyer. And when a minute or two later he

declared that he had taken the liberty of calling
only for the sake of inquiring after the Signorina
Regina, and that he must be now starting on his
way home to Sponda Lunga, the farmer, after
replying very heartily and graciously to his inquiries, said that he would walk a bit of the way
with him.

" But it is just supper time, Signor Giovanni," urged the lawyer ; " won't you come up
stairs to supper ? "

The mere possibility of coming to be the master
of ten thousand crowns had made a sensible
difference also in the farmer's estimate of and
feeling towards Carlo.   The lawyer perceived
instantly that it was so, and considered it quite
a matter of course that it should be so.   But it
made him feel a sort of jealousy and special un-
willingness that the farmer and Carlo should
have such an opportunity for tête-a-tête talk.
Signor Giacomo Morini had been working very
hard to do away with the unfavourable impression his son had made upon the farmer by his
conduct in the matter of the Sponda Lunga
robbery, with very little success.   And he

dreaded that under this impression, and moved also by the dazzling vision of the ten thousand dollars, illusory though it would probably prove to be, the farmer might be led into making some promise to Carlo, which might make his son's course more difficult.

But the farmer was not to be driven from his purpose so easily.

" Never mind the supper, neighbour," he said, in answer to the lawyer's remark. " I don't feel inclined for supper to-night, and I want to have a bit of talk with Signor Carlo."

It was a signal and rare mark of the farmer's favour to be called Signor " Carlo." Generally Signor Bartoli did not accord him any such admission of equality and friendship, but addressed him by the more distant, Signor Caroli. It is always complimentary to an Italian to address him by his Christian name.

So the farmer and Carlo left the lawyer's studio together.

" Well, this *is* a wonderful history ! " began the farmer, as soon as ever they were in the street,—" wonderful ! I should not wonder if you recovered the money, *figliuolo mio!*   Ten thousand crowns is a big mouthful to swallow without people seeing that you have anything out of common in your mouth.   Do you think there is any hope of it yourself, Signor Carlo?'

" Well, Signor Giovanni, the truth is I did not want to say anything about it before Signor Morini . . . . ."

" No! you're right there! lawyers you know . . . . they make mischief as often as they mend it.   Like the tinkers—mend one hole and make two! " said the farmer, confidentially,

" Well, the fact is, that I can't help thinking that our priest himself knows something more about the money than he chooses to admit," said Carlo.   And then he told the farmer all the story of the bogy that had frightened little Beppina Trilli,—the manner and circumstances of his mother's death,—and the probability that the time when she fell on the steps must have been much about the same hour that little Beppina saw the bogy.   He also told the farmer that the Rev. Pasquale Mommi did not enjoy a perfectly immaculate reputation, and men-

tioned the intention of the Pescia Commissary to
search the reverend gentleman's premises.

"By the *Santissimo Volto Santo,* I'd wager
a trifle that he has got the money. Let a priest
alone for being down on the dollars, wherever
there are any! And if he has got the money
you'll get it back again! Of course you will!
He can't have made away with it so soon," said
the farmer, rubbing his hands in great glee.
He was already contemplating all the advantages of having a son-in-law with TEN THOUSAND
DOLLARS in ready cash. Make an offer for
Ripalta; buy it dirt cheap under present circumstances, when the owner is suddenly called
on to make a considerable outlay. What could
not be done with *ten thousand dollars* down?

" No ! he hardly could have made away with
it," said Carlo ; " but, even if he has got it,
which we have no right to take for granted, he
may likely enough have hidden it, where the
police can't find it."

" They are great hands at finding anything
they choose to look for," said the farmer ;—
"great hands. And specially when they that are

to be looked up have no suspicion that the police is a going to pay them a visit. I am very glad the Commissary was so sharp about it—so as to give him no time to be put up to it any way. I wonder you did not stay at Pescia, Signor Carlo, to hear the upshot of the search."

" Well, Signor Giovanni, they did not want me there up at Uzzano; and to tell you the truth I was very anxious to be at home here. I felt that to be away just at present might seem as if I was ashamed to show my face, and that those who suspect me of dishonesty might think that my going away looked as if I were conscious of guilt. It was a great sorrow to me to be obliged to go at all!" added Carlo, with a deep sigh.

" Don't you fret about it, *figliuolo mio.* You mark my words, it will be found out who stole those dollars. The lawyer there is honest, though between ourselves I don't think he would ha' been sorry if it had been you that stole the widow's money. And as for his son .... I never was so disgusted with a fellow in my life! Perhaps you don't know, Signor Carlo,

that it was he that sent the police officers out
to the widow's house that day—all out of his
head, for all the world just like one of their own
paid spies. I could not have believed such a
thing if anybody except the fellow himself had
told me of it. Goes straight off to the office,
and tells them all about it, letting them think
they were sent for by the widow. Ugh! "

"I thought as much," said Carlo, telling the
truth, but not the whole truth. "I thought as
much; but I had no objection to their coming
out. The more inquiry the better for me."

"Ay, ay! that's all very well, but it's no
excuse for him, a dirty, malicious, little black-
guard of an informer. There's no more friendship between Meo Morini and me, nor never will
be!" said the farmer, meaningly, "Did the
police Commissary at Pescia seem to think there
was a chance of catching the real thieves?" he
asked.

"Why, yes; I think he did, when I told him
about . . . . all about the thing as it happened,"
said Carlo, recollecting just before he uttered the
words on the tip of his tongue, that it was only

from Regina's letter that he then knew of the marking of the money.

" Yes ; and depend on it, it will .... and then .... well, good-night, Signor Carlo," said the farmer, checking himself in his turn. " Good-night, and a pleasant walk to you.   Come in again before long, and let us hear all about it, and how matters are going on."

" Good-night, Signor Giovanni ; give my compliments to the Signorina Regina," said Carlo, shaking hands with the old man cordially.

" Compliments ! " said the farmer ; " compliments be damned.   I don't suppose Regina would say just that," he added, with a broad laugh ; " but mayhap she would think it.   When a man has saved a girl's life, he may send her something a trifle warmer than compliments."

" Oh, signore !   *Troppo buono !* " muttered Carlo, colouring up to the roots of his hair, and feeling as if he hardly knew whether he stood on his head or his heels.   " La Signorina ....
Regina .... I am sure .... pray say that .... that .... I mean .... tell her that .... I hope .... I hope soon to have the

great pleasure of . . . . of thanking her for her
kindness in person . . . . if I may take that
liberty ! "

" To be sure, come and see her ! She don't
believe you were ever a thief, I can tell you ! "
said the farmer.

And so the two men parted, the farmer to go
back to Lucca, and Carlo to continue his walk
to Sponda Lunga ;—the former meditating whether mayhap his young friend, if it should come
to pass that he found himself suddenly in possession of such a fortune as ten thousand crowns,
might feel inclined to look higher for a wife than
his daughter ;—the latter feeling as if his ears
must have played him some trick in conveying
to his brain the purport of the farmer's last
words. Surely it was hardly possible to mistake the drift of them, if he had heard them
aright ! Surely the farmer must have meant
him to understand that he would willingly have
him for a son-in-law ! Signor Giovanni bidding
him to send something warmer than compliments to his daughter !—pressing him to
come and see her !—and that under circum-

stances which to him had seemed to make it
unfitting that he should venture to call on her !
Could it be possible that the mere sound of this
ten thousand dollars,—the mere chance of
coming into such a fortune could have worked
this wonder ! It was true that, as he was
aware, the farmer had altogether broken with
Meo Morini, before he had heard anything
about the prize in the lottery ;—true that the
service he had been able to render to Regina
had brought forth lively expressions of gratitude
from her father. But . . . !

If Carlo could have read the entire contents
of the farmer's heart, he would have seen,
firstly, a real generous liking for himself engen-
dered by what he had done on the night of the
flood ; secondly, a real generous disgust at the
baseness of Meo Morini ; thirdly, a certain half-
acknowledged feeling, that it would save a vast
amount of sorrow and trouble, and make un-
necessary a fight, in which, despite his bold
front, he did not feel comfortably sure that he
should be the victor, if Regina's wishes and his
own could be found compatible in the matter of

choosing a husband for her; and, fourthly, a very lively perception of the advantages of having a son-in-law with *ten thousand crowns* DOWN; together with a very strong persuasion that the sum in question would be recovered.

CHAPTER III.

EVERYTHING moves slowly in Tuscany; and at the date of this story was wont to move more slowly still. Everything connected with the public administration of affairs moved more slowly than the matters pertaining to any other department of life. And police investigations (when concerned merely with the private affairs and interests of the citizens) moved most slowly of all.

It was several days, therefore, before anything more was heard of the inquiries which had been set on foot respecting the two suspected robberies, that at Sponda Lunga, and that at Uzzano, by any of the parties concerned. And one of these parties, who was interested in both inquiries, Carlo Caroli, began to despair of any result from either.

He was not, however, without comfort and consolation during these weary and anxious days. For, greatly as Farmer Bartoli's unmistakeable advances had taken him by surprise, and left him in such a whirl of excitement and emotion, that it seemed to him at first that he should not be able to venture on acting upon the invitation which had been given him, he arose the next morning, not only determined to pay a visit to the lawyer's house in Lucca that very day, but counting the hours till the day should be sufficiently advanced for him to do so. Whether by fortunate chance, or by arrangement planned by the farmer himself, he found everything exactly as he would have wished. On asking for the Signorina Bartoli, he was told to go upstairs to the sitting-room. How his heart beat as he sprung up the narrow and steep old stone staircase four steps at a bound ! He opened the door of the room indicated to him, fully expecting to find himself confronted by the Signora Morini, perhaps alone, perhaps

accompanied by Regina. And what an awkward, disagreeable mode of meeting that would
be !

But no! there was Regina, and Regina
alone !

For the first five minutes of their interview
the conversation was carried on in a manner
which might, perhaps, be satisfactorily described
by an intelligent system of hieroglyphics, but
which is not readily rendered by the resources
of an ordinary fount of type. And when, sub-
siding from that first phase of the interchange
of thought and feeling, their intercommunion
flowed in a less interrupted stream of discourse,
it was such that it hardly seems necessary to
give a verbatim report of it. There may be
readers who would be altogether at a loss to
conceive what Carlo Caroli and Regina Bartoli
said to each other. But it is scarcely to be
expected that such will be among *my* readers.
None of those, I take it, who may be tempted
to peruse this narrative, will be at any loss to
guess what passed between them. All their
hopes and fears were discussed with entire

open-heartedness between them. All that the
farmer had said was weighed and commented
on. There was one little word only that
Regina could not bring herself to repeat to ·
Caroli, of all her father had said. She could
not tell him that her father had dropped words
which seemed to intimate a doubt whether
Caroli, in possession of ten thousand dollars,
would be as eager a suitor as Caroli without a
soldo in his pocket. Regina, who knew very
well that the possession of ten millions of
dollars would have made no difference either to
his or to her love, could not frame words to say
this. The chances of the recovery of this
money were discussed between them, however,
and the advantages of it fully admitted and
appreciated. It was admitted that the farmer's
readiness to accept Carlo as a son-in-law might
be expected to be much influenced by this con-
tingency. And it was stoutly upheld by Carlo
himself that the entire and complete clearing
of his name from every shade of suspicion in
connection with the robbery of the widow's
money must precede any application to her

father for permission to ask her hand. But Regina persisted in being hopeful on both these points. She would not admit that it could be doubtful for a minute that Carlo would eventually be proved to have had nothing to do with the robbery which had certainly been committed at Sponda Lunga. And she owned to a very comfortable persuasion that the ten thousand dollars would be recovered.

In short, whenever Carlo was inclined to despond, she was bravely ready to comfort and to cheer him with hopeful words and arguments.

And then her delivery from the dreadful Meo! Had not her Carlo accomplished that for her already? The day would come when that blessed release would be the only remaining consequence of the circumstances that had fallen out so untowardly at Sponda Lunga! And how they rejoiced together over this great deliverance!

But the envious hours ran by the while! If poor mad Nat Lee's prayer to the gods to "annihilate but space and time, and make two lovers happy," has never yet been granted,

lovers take their revenge by wholly disregard-
ing one at least of those stern adversaries!
Time may tramp on in his Juggernaut course
as doggedly as he will. They heed not his
moving!—heed it not till pulled up with more
or less sharpness by some importunate reminder
of the mere mortal impediments they had
forgotten.

In the case in hand, surly old Time's agent
for this odious reminder was Aurora,—not she
of the rosy fingers, importunate reminder as
she is apt to be!—but Aurora, the withered
little old woman, who did the house service in
the establishment of Signor Morini, and who
came clattering into the room with plates and
glasses to prepare for the family dinner!

"Good gracious, Carlo, why it is dinner-
time! It seems impossible. I could not have
believed it!"

Carlo looked at his watch in amazement, and
confirmed the wonderful fact that it was more
than three hours since they had met!

"We have had so many things to talk of,
you see, Carlo! That's how it is! Now they

will be coming in, some of them, in a minute.
I wish father would come in first, that you
might say a word to him. But he will be sure
to come with Signor Morini, and most likely
that horrid Meo will be with them! You had
better go!"

"I suppose I had better! I don't want to
meet Signor Meo. *Addio, Regina mia!* Mine
once again!"

"Not a bit of it;—again! There is no
again, Carlo! Yours, as I told you that night,
when we stood at the widow's door without a
dry rag on either of us, yours once and always,
then, ever since then, now and for ever!"

And so they parted. But Carlo, having thus
found his way into the lawyer's house, did not
allow many days to pass before he came again.
And in this way the weary days were made
less intolerable to his anxiety.

At last, one morning as he was setting out
from Sponda Lunga to walk to Lucca, he met a
man who accosted him, and told him that he
was sent by the Commissary of Police to request
the attendance of Signor Carlo Caroli at the

police court on the following day at twelve.
And having delivered this message *vivâ voce*,
he reinforced it by handing Carlo a paper
with a printed form filled up to the same
effect.

At last, then, it was to be hoped that something had been discovered! But which of the
two matters, in both of which he was so deeply
interested, did it concern? Carlo eagerly
hoped it might have reference to the robbery at
Sponda Lunga. To come into ten thousand
crowns was a great matter. But to be freed
from the horrible cloud that had hung over
him and made his life loathsome to him for
many a weary day, was a greater still.

That day the talk between him and Regina
was mainly occupied with the conjectures,
hopes, and fears, elicited by this invitation for
the morrow. Regina was able to tell Carlo
that she had heard that Signor Morini had
received a similar invitation for the same hour
on the morrow. And this seemed to indicate
that the matter in hand was the Sponda Lunga
robbery. For it was difficult to imagine what

connection the Lucca lawyer could have with the other affair.

Carlo thought that the remaining hours of that day, and of the night that followed it, would never pass away. But he had at hand, during many of those hours, a comforter as eager to console him as Regina herself. The kind widow, too, had store of endless arguments to prove that all would go well. They were, in all probability, logically as cogent as those of Regina. But somehow they did not seem to Carlo to have the same convincing and consoling effect.

However, the hours went by, as hours will go, if one is only patient with them ; and at a little before twelve o'clock on the next day Carlo found himself at the door of the police office in Lucca.

There had been some other invitations issued to this pleasant little meeting at the office of the Commissary of Police for the city of Lucca, besides the two that have been already mentioned. Signore Andrea Simonetti had received one also. But though he had accepted it, as such invita-

tions *are* usually accepted, he had by no means
done so with the same joyful alacrity with
which our friend Carlo had responded to the
call.

In fact, Signor Andrea did not like it at all.
Ever since that question about the ownership of
the pocket-handkerchief, he had been in a state
of nervous uneasiness, which manifested itself
by a morose snappishness towards all around
him.   His sister,—the same who had so inopportunely, as it had seemed to her brother,
compelled him, by her officious testimony, to
admit that the handkerchief was his,—had on
several occasions roused his ire by recurring to
the subject of it.   She could not be content to
acquiesce in the loss of an article of property.
She remarked that the police had sufficiently
assured themselves that it was his ; yet they
did not return it.   She wondered whether her
brother was going to put up with being robbed
in that way.   For her part, if it were *her* affair
she would let the police have no rest till they
were shamed into giving the property up !   All
which remarks of his sister seemed to be

very especially distasteful to her brother. He damned the handkerchief with concentrated bitterness ; never wanted to be bothered about the cursed rag any more ; and bade his sister mind her own business, with great asperity.

And now at last had come the intimation that the Commissary of Police wished to speak with Signor Andrea Simonetti ! Andrea turned very pale when the message was communicated to him at his desk in his father's little office, if "pale" can be held to describe the colour which yellow, bloodless faces turn under the influence of terror.

"More trouble," he said, "about that cursed handkerchief ! It is very hard that when a fellow has been robbed, and would rather put up with his loss than waste valuable time over it, he should be harassed in this way. Damn the Commissary ! I shall not go to him."

"Oh, you had better go, Andrea !" his father had said. " They won't be beat that way ; and the first trouble is the least."

And Andrea did present himself at the office at the hour named, which was the same as that for which Carlo and the lawyer had been invited.

A stranger to Tuscan ways might have judged, from the manner in which this invitation had been delivered and the words in which it was conceived, that there could be nothing in the cause of the summons of a nature to render the person so invited *very* unwilling to obey the call. But Signor Andrea Simonetti had no such comfortable persuasion. He knew the ways of that department of the social system of his country too well to indulge in any such notion. In very many cases in which an English magistrate would proceed by a warrant for arrest, the Tuscan magistrate contents himself with the milder-seeming " Ducky, ducky, come and be killed ! " method of procedure. He knows,—or knew rather, for I am speaking of a past order of things,—that in a country where nobody could indulge in locomotion without a passport, it was hardly likely, except perhaps in the case of desperate criminals, that the person he summoned should attempt to run away instead of coming to the summons. He knew

that his arms were very long in proportion to
the use which any citizen could make of his
legs. And, in point of fact, such invitations
were in practice always found sufficient to
attain the object in view.

Signor Andrea Simonetti accordingly at-
tended at the time and place named. The
first thing he saw at the door was the man
he hated most in all the world, evidently
come on a similar errand to himself. The
presence of Caroli seemed to him to augur
nothing good! What the devil could *he* be
wanted for in any matter connected with himself! Signor Andrea had nobody to make that
remark to at the moment, and so, oddly enough
as it might seem, he made it to himself! His
heart misgave him as to the connection which
it was possible to suppose Caroli might have
with the matter in hand. He could not really
deceive himself. And yet, so strangely are
men constituted, he sought a certain amount of
comfort in lying to himself.

The two men's eyes inadvertently met; but
Andrea turned away without any salutation,

with an affectation of making this cut direct as
marked and visible to all bystanders as possible.
Carlo entered the door of the place first, and
ascended the dirty staircase.

CHAPTER IV.

NOTHING can be conceived more squalid than
the appearance of such places in Italian cities.
The door, in a back street, was just like the
door of any of the neighbouring houses, save
that it was marked by a little bit of board,
painted with the arms of the Grand Duchy,
over the door, and by sundry printed forms
pasted up on the doorposts and on each side of
them. The door opened on a narrow dark
passage. On one side of this, another door
opened into a small room, where there was a
sort of glazed closet in one corner, in which three
young men sate, holding little earthenware
pots, filled with burning braise, in their hands,
and apparently doing nothing whatever. The
table or desk in front of them was begrimed all

over with a mixture of ink and sand ;—the
sand used for drying fresh writing. Around
the bare walls of the room were ranged narrow
wooden benches painted yellow. And on these
were lounging one or two men, officials of some
sort apparently, half asleep, and an old country-
man, looking the personification of patient
waiting.

The persons summoned for an interview with
the Commissary, however, had no business with
the denizens of this outer court of the temple of
Themis. The stone stair by which Carlo went
up to the first floor, passing by this room, was
long, narrow, and very dirty. It brought him
to a large open landing place dirtier and more
squalid-looking still, in one corner of which was
another little glazed closet, in which one or two
men were sitting. Two or three other officials,
of the nature of ushers of the court, messengers
or so forth, marked as such by some fragment
of red cloth let in to the collars of their coats,
were lounging about. There was an air of super-
lative seediness and sauntering idleness about
these men passing the seediness and the idleness

of any other seedy and idle men.   There was
an unwholesome look about them suggestive of
lives passed in some dark and close cellars ; and
there was a nauseous smell of closeness and
mephitic sordidness pervading the entire place.
It suggested the conceit that knavery must
be odorous ; and that all the rogues, who for
years past had been within those walls, had
left behind them the scent of their heteroge-
neous villanies, which had never been diluted
by any admixture of the atmosphere from
without.

Here also there were narrow yellow benches
round the walls, on which a singularly hetero-
geneous assemblage of people were waiting with
that impassible, inexhaustible, and apparently perfectly contented patience, which so peculiarly cha-
racterizes the Tuscan people.   There were decent-
looking countrymen of the peasant class ; spe-
cimens of the most ragged ruffianism of the
city ; old women holding huge umbrellas in their
hands, and big baskets after the manner of uni-
versal old-womanhood.   There was nothing by
which anybody could guess whether these people

were accusers or accused, or witnesses. They con-
versed with each other in whispers, and every now
and then one would rise from his seat, and step
to one of the three or four doors which opened
on this landing-place or ante-chamber, and
which stood ajar, peep through it, and return
impassible to his or her seat. Some others were
standing about the floor of the place, and these
had mostly the air of belonging to a somewhat
higher grade in the social scale. Among these
latter, Carlo, on entering, saw Signor Giacomo
Morini, the lawyer.

No one of the officials accosted Carlo when
he came in, or seemed to take the smallest
notice of him. The lawyer, who had an air of
being at home there, and of knowing all the
ways of the place, bowed to him with the cheerful semblance of one who welcomes another to a
pleasant gathering, but said no word bearing on
the business which both must have had in their
thoughts.

" Ha, Signor Caroli ! A fine morning ! The
mornings are getting sharp, now ; but it is
lovely weather for a walk from Sponda Lunga.

I trust you left our friend, the widow Monaldi, well ! "

A minute after Signor Simonetti entered, and was greeted by the lawyer in similar fashion. He seemed less at his ease than all the rest of the assembly. His eye was restless, and seemed to be continually scanning the crowd in search of somebody or something. And either from finding or from not finding what he was looking for, he seemed to become somewhat more reassured.

At length after waiting, what to an impatient Englishman would have seemed an interminable and intolerable time, but which in no one of the Italians assembled appeared to cause the smallest symptom of impatience, one of the officials before mentioned made a slight motion of his head, or rather of his eyes only, towards Lawyer Morini, there was a slight stir in the room, the lawyer in similar manner telegraphed to Caroli and to Simonetti, the official nodded towards one of the doors, and the two young men and the lawyer passed in through it, while those left outside contentedly composed themselves for another hour or so of waiting.

It was a large and lofty room into which they entered, once the outer chamber of a suite of reception rooms in the palace of some Lucchese noble ;—now very bare, very bleak, very dirty, and very imperfectly lighted. At the further end of it a small space was railed off, and behind the rails on a slightly raised dais were three little tables covered with green baize. And behind each little table there was a chair. But the chairs were empty; and it was evident that no business was being transacted in the court at that time.

Lawyer Morini, however, led the way across the large hall to a door in the side of it, through which, with his two companions, he passed into a smaller and more habitable-looking room, lined with bookshelves filled with what seemed to be not books, but large folio bundles of papers collected into book-covers, and lettered at the back with dates in large black ink letters. Here, also, were two small tables, covered with green baize, one on each side of the empty fire-place. At one of these sat an elderly gentleman, having before him a confused mass of written papers, all materials for writing, and a large wooden bowl of sand, with droppings from which all the table and the things on it were grimy.

There was no fire in the fire-place ; but the occupant of the room held down between his knees, under the table, a *scaldino*, or little earthenware pot, full of lighted braise, which, after a slight bow and a word or two of recognition, he offered to Signor Morini, who accepted the courtesy.

The Commissary—for it was the principal Commissary of Police for the city and district of Lucca, in person—motioned to his three visitors to be seated on the rush-bottomed chairs which were placed on the opposite side of the table to his own, and proceeded to open the business in hand.

To Carlo's great surprise and disappointment, —apparently also to the surprise of Lawyer Morini,—the Commissary did not say a word about the robbery at Sponda Lunga. Nor did the matter on which he did enter seem to have any connection with that. Carlo began to imagine

that it was the fashion of the place to call into
the august presence in which he found himself,
two different cases at a time.

The Commissary produced a handkerchief, *the*
handkerchief which Clorinda Simonetti had
marked with her own hands, and which she had
so emphatically declared to belong to her
brother.

" This handkerchief is your property, I believe, Signor Andrea Simonetti ? " began the
Commissary.

Simonetti assented, sullenly and evidently ill
at ease.

" How came it out of your possession ? "

" I don't know, Signor Commissario. How
should I know ? I suppose it was stolen from
my pocket. I know nothing about it. It is a
common accident enough," replied Simonetti.

" It is, unfortunately. However, we have
found the handkerchief for you," said the Commissary, drily.

Simonetti put out his hand to take the recovered property.

" Not yet ! You must be content to leave it

in our hands for awhile, if you please. It shall
be taken care of. Have you no idea who could
have stolen it from you ? "

" None at all, Signor Commissario. I have
told you so," said the young man, sulkily.

" We have reason to think that it was stolen
from your pocket at Leghorn, by one Pasquale
or Pasqualuccio Curbi, domiciled at Leghorn,"
said the Commissary, eyeing him keenly.

" What of it, if it was ? What does that
prove ? " said Simonetti, turning visibly pale.
" I mean, that is, that at all events it could not
have been stolen at Leghorn, for it is long since
I have been there. Of course the man you
speak of, may have stolen it elsewhere. It is all
one to me, *where* he did it. But I think it is
very hard that I should be put to so much
trouble about it."

" I am sorry for any trouble we may be
obliged to give you, signor. But the fact is
that it does matter to other people, and I am
sorry to say to you also, *where* that handkerchief was stolen, and I will not conceal from
you that we have strong reason to think that it

was taken from your pocket at Leghorn, and in the house of this Pasquale Curbi."

Carlo had ceased to pay any attention to the above conversation as soon as it seemed clear to him that it had no reference to his own affairs. His mind was fully occupied with the question which he supposed would occupy the Commissary's attention as soon as Signor Simonetti's business should be despatched. The lawyer, more experienced in such matters, had listened with a surprised and puzzled interest. But the attention of both of them was now called to Simonetti. He seemed to be on the point of fainting. His face, even to his lips, was livid, and he supported himself on his chair with difficulty.

" Take a glass of water, Signor Simonetti," said the Commissary, pouring one out from the carafe which stood on a shelf behind his table, and offering it to him ; " you find the room close, perhaps."

"Yes ! it is rather close ! that is the fact ! " said the young man, recovering himself with a great effort as he took the proffered glass of water with a shaking hand and drank the contents eagerly. "I am right enough!" he continued, putting the glass down; "but, as I told you, Signor Commissario, if the handkerchief was stolen from my pocket, it could not have been stolen at Leghorn; and if it was stolen at Leghorn, it was stolen from some other pocket than mine. For I have not been at Leghorn—that is certain. Why, these things get lost at the wash ;—changed ;—sent home to the wrong person ;—it happens every day!"

"Yes! oh, yes! no doubt! But I am afraid, Signor Simonetti, that that handkerchief was stolen from your pocket in the house of Pasquale Curbi, at Leghorn, a very short time ago. Do you mean to say that you have not been there?"

"At Leghorn! a short time ago! certainly not! Everybody at our house knows I have not been there! There's the clerks,—two of them. They know where I am all day! They can be examined on oath! Certainly I deny that I have been at Leghorn for a long time back."

"Perhaps, signor, the clerks may know where

you are, as you say, all day, but not *all night!*
Can you deny, now, that you were at Leghorn
on the night previous to the robbery in the
widow Monaldi's house at Sponda Lunga?"

"Most certainly I can, and do deny it!"
returned Simonetti at once; "and can prove
that I was not there that night!"

"What night?" said the Commissary.

"Why, the night you said—the night before
the robbery at the widow Monaldi's house!"
cried Simonetti.

"Oh, then, you know what night that was!
That will be valuable information to us. Nobody has been able to discover, hitherto, on
what night—or day—the robbery took place,"
said the Commissary.

Again the wretched young man seemed like
to fall in collapse on the floor. His white lips
moved without speaking, and he trembled all
over. Again, however, he made a violent effort
to nerve himself with the reflection that there
was no proof of any sort against him. He
rose from his seat, as if to shake off the weight
that oppressed him.

"I don't know what you mean, Signor Commissario," he said; "you confuse me so by asking about a lot of things that I know nothing about! Of course I don't know any more than you do when the robbery at Sponda Lunga happened. Of course I don't; how should I?"

Carlo and the lawyer had been listening to the latter part of this with increasing interest and surprise. It appeared abundantly clear to the former, from the manner of Simonetti, that he was guilty of something in some way; but he could not imagine how the stealing of Signor Simonetti's handkerchief could have any bearing on the robbery at the widow's, and still less how it could have any such bearing as to connect that person with it as a guilty party. Even the lawyer was altogether puzzled at the turn matters seemed to be taking.

"Well, then, Signor Simonetti, since you decline to admit having made any such excursion to Leghorn, I must tell you that the ostler at the stables at San Martino declares that you hired a *bagarino* and pony . . ."

"Yes! I remember that very well! I had

business at Monte Catini ;—a commission for
my father, which I had forgotten. I remember
mentioning it to the man who let me the
bagarino ! ”

“ Yes ! you mentioned that to the man. But
then the ostler of the *Tre piccioni* outside the
gate at Leghorn declares that you put up there
that same night . . .”

“But you have not yet done me the favour
to mention, Signor Commissario,” said Simonetti,
feeling with a sense of sickening terror that the
net was closing round him, but determined to
struggle to the last ;—“ you have not yet been
kind enough to tell me why I should not go to
Leghorn, if I so choose ;—nay, why I should
not, if I choose, wish to keep my going a secret !
Diamine ! There are reasons, it seems to me,
why a man may wish not to publish to all the
world every little excursion he may make, and
yet his reasons may not much matter to the
police ! ”

“ Certainly ! certainly ! signore ; and I would
not be guilty of indiscretion on such a subject
for all the world ! Nevertheless, on this occa-

sion, I must ask you, since it seems that we may take it as admitted that you were at Leghorn on the night in question, what was the business which took you there ?"

"I do not understand that I can be called upon to answer any such questions,—put to me, too, without being told why they are asked. I do not admit that I was at Leghorn! Nor will I answer any questions on the subject! *Che diavolo!* Am I to be put on the rack, as used to be the fashion once upon a time with you gentlemen of the police ?"

"No! signore! not at all. But—having taken note of the answers you have given, as well as of the points on which you refuse to answer, I must proceed to let you hear what another person has to say on these same matters."

And so saying, the Commissary rang a bell, the handle of which was close to his little table.

"Let Michele Landi, *detto il Moro,* come in !" said the Commissario to the attendant who answered the bell.

And in a minute or two in walked Signor

Simonetti's and the reader's old acquaintance, Michele Landi, the Carbonaio of Leghorn!

Simonetti started, as if he had seen the fiend in person enter the room; and he visibly staggered under the blow thus unexpectedly dealt him. It was evident to him that in some way or other the actual perpetrators of the Sponda Lunga robbery had been discovered. But still it remained to be seen whether the police were in possession of any real proof of his complicity in the crime.

He was not left long in doubt. Michele Landi, dealer in charcoal, commonly called " Il Moro," was, as the reader has had an opportunity of observing, a man of more natural intelligence, and, in a certain degree, and a certain sense, of greater culture than his more ruffianly friend, Pasqualuccio. He was one of those men who lend a show of reason to the theories, now happily pretty well obsolete, by virtue of which it used to be maintained that a certain measure of education only served to make the dangerous classes more dangerous. Michele Landi could read and write. Pasqualuccio Curbi could do neither. And Michele was unquestionably the deeper-dyed scoundrel of the two. He was a man of the Talleyrand type, with brains enough to comprehend and feel a contempt for his own worthlessness, compensated to him and made tolerable by a belief in the equal worthlessness of all around him, a cynicism without which complete unredeemed and unredeemable scoundrelism is hardly attained. These are the men who most notably confute that other silly theory of there being " honour among thieves."

Michele Landi, the Carbonaio, entered the Commissary's room with an air of perfect ease and self-possession. He was much better dressed than on the occasion of Simonetti's interview with him in his own cellar; and to anyone not skilled in the book of the human countenance might have seemed a respectable and well-to-do artisan.

The Commissary did not offer to him the courtesy which he had shown to the others there assembled of inviting him to be seated, and he remained standing with perfect nonchalance near the door.

"Now, Michele Landi," said the Commissary, "I must ask you to repeat,—not for the last time, I am afraid,—the story you have already told more than once. The best way of doing so will be by replying to my questions."

"*Si, signore!*" said the fellow, with an easy bow, and a smiling glance at each one of his audience.

"Have you any acquaintance with either of these gentlemen?"

"*'Gnor, si!* I have the honour of being well acquainted with the Signorino Andrea Simonetti. I am not aware of having ever seen either of these other gentlemen before."

"When and where did you last see Signor Andrea Simonetti?"

"It was about three weeks ago, or rather more, I think, that I had the honour of receiving Signor Andrea in my own poor residence in Leghorn. It was between one and two o'clock in the morning. I have not had the pleasure of seeing the gentleman since that time. He was accompanied to my retired place of abode by another valued friend of mine, the Signor Pasquale Curbi."

"Now relate, if you please, what took place at that interview."

"I am sorry to interrupt you, Signor Commissario," broke in Simonetti, "and it is perfectly indifferent to me what tissue of lies this man may have made up. But you will understand that it is due to myself to protest at once against any credit being given to any story coming from such a source."

"Quite so, Signor Simonetti, quite so! I will take note of your protest,—noting, at the same time, the admission involved in it, that you have some knowledge of Signor Michele Landi," said the Commissary.

Simonetti frowned heavily, and bit his white lips;—then opened them as if about to speak. But he checked himself, and said nothing. Michele looked at him with one of those inimitable Italian shrugs, not of the shoulders only, but of the eyes, face, mouth, and entire person, which, put into words, would have said with the utmost good humour, "What would you have?

We are in a mess, and must make, each of us, the best we can of it."

"You were going to tell us what passed at the last interview you had with Signor Simonetti," resumed the Commissary.

"*Si, signore!* Signor Andrea mentioned that it was in his power to do my friend Pasquale and myself the kindness of pointing out to us a certain sum of five hundred dollars, which it would be very easy for us to appropriate to our own needs by the simple process of taking it. That *was* kind. But I am free to confess, signore, that my experience of the world does not lead me to put much trust in the kindness of any creature walking on two legs and with a tongue in his head. And my opinions on this point led me to inquire of Signor Simonetti what *his* interest in the matter was,—what he was to gain by the robbery of this sum of money. Signor Simonetti is, I dare say, free from the fault of being too frank in general. But he is frank to his friends. He saw at once the justice of my demand; and he told us, with perfect frank-

ness, that his object in the matter was the ruin
of a certain man who had the charge of this
money, and who would necessarily be considered to be the thief,—one Carlo Caroli!"

Caroli started to his feet, and was about to
speak ; but the Commissary, with a rapid
warning motion of his hand, signed to him to
re-seat himself and be silent. The lawyer,
Morini, stretched out his legs before him, threw
himself back in his chair, and turned his face
up towards the ceiling with an expression of
devout horror at the wickedness of mankind in
general.

"I believe," continued the Queen's evidence,
as we should call him, "I think that Signor
Andrea was good enough to enter into some
explanation of his special reasons for hating this
Carlo Caroli. But I can't say that I paid any
such attention to this part of his communication
as to have remembered it. It was no business
of mine. It was enough that he hated this
man, to make me understand what I wanted to
understand,—why Signor Andrea wished the
money to be stolen, without getting a *soldo* of

it himself. And when Signor Andrea spoke of his hatred for this Caroli, there was no mistake about it that he was telling the truth! *That* was truth, if he never spoke another true word in his life. *I* didn't want to know *why* he hated him. *Che vuole!* what would you have? Men *do* hate each other—sometimes."

"Never mind your philosophy, Signor Landi! we can dispense with that," said the Commissary. "Go on and tell us what followed at the interview between you and Signor Simonetti."

And then the man went on to detail, with great exactitude and perfect coolness, all the information given to him and his accomplice by Simonetti,—the impression of the key, and the instructions how to find the trick of the secret hiding-place, ending with a relation of the manner in which the robbery had been carried into effect with complete success.

While he spoke, a dead, dogged despair had been gradually settling down upon Simonetti. When the story was ended, and the Commissary, turning gravely to him, asked if there was any further observation he thought fit to

make on the evidence which had been given,
he said, in a hoarse voice that seemed quite
different from that in which he had previously
spoken :

"I have said already that I protest against
any credit being given to the mass of lies
concocted, evidently, by this man in order to
save himself by having a story to tell the
police."

"All those considerations will, doubtless,
have their due weight in proper time and
place," replied the Commissary ; "but I may
observe to you now, that we should not have
given such credit to the avowals of this man as
to have proceeded to the step of arresting you,
had there not been in the circumstances of the
case abundant corroborating evidences."

"Arrest, Signor Commissario ! You surely
do not mean to say that you mean to detain me
on the faith of this story ? "

"I am grieved to say, Signor Simonetti, that
it will be my painful duty to do so ! "

"What, now ? Do you mean that I am not
to be permitted to return to my home ? " said

the miserable wretch, while the cold perspiration broke out in large drops on his forehead.

"If you wish to return to your home for a short time,—a few minutes,—you can do so in the company of an officer. But the gravity of the case will not justify me in permitting you to continue at large. Do you wish to return to your house for the purpose of arranging any matters with your family?"

"No! I am not going to be marched through the streets in the custody of an officer, like a deserter from the army. No! you may do your worst, Signor Commissario! You have the upper hand now! Perhaps it may not be so always. *Chi vivra verra!*"

"Good morning, gentlemen!" said Michele, as he and Simonetti followed a couple of *giandarmi*, who appeared outside the door when it was opened. "You will excuse my friend Signor Andrea for losing his temper a little! He has had the game all his own way so much hitherto, that he's got crusty at a turn of fortune! Come, Signor Andrea! Don't fret and fume about it! You can't always have it all your own way! *Che diavolo!*"

The three men who remained in the room when the usurer's son and Landi left it, looked at each other in silence for a minute or so. The Commissary, rising from his table and standing with his back to the empty fireplace, plunged his hands deep into his pockets and nodded his head slowly up and down, while looking into the lawyer's eyes, with protruded under lip.

"A very ugly bit of business!" he said at length;—"as ugly a bit of business as I have had in my hands for many a day. Signor Caroli, I congratulate you on being entirely freed from what was a very disagreeable position. Signor Morini, you have yet to learn why I requested you to come here this morning. If I am rightly informed, you can give evidence as to certain marks on these dollars?" he said, taking two crowns from a paper on his table.

Morini took the dollars and examined them.

"Yes!" he said, "I can testify that those two

dollars were part of the money,—five hundred dollars—sent by me to the widow Monaldi by my son ; . . . unless, indeed, one of them be a dollar I lent to the Brigadier, to help him in his investigations."

"No! the Brigadier has that still in his keeping. These are two of the dollars stolen from the widow Monaldi. It was the mark that put us on the scent ;—and it was quite a piece of luck after all."

"How was it, then, Signor Commissario ? " asked Morini.

" Why, this was it. These two worthies, on the night following the robbery at Sponda Lunga, stole a valuable old silver goblet from a house near Pescia. The goblet was a special one,— the work of some celebrated artist,—*che so io!* But it was an article easy to trace. It was discovered in the shop of one Stefano Gralli, on the jewellers' bridge at Florence. The first thing we did with your bit of marked money, signore, was to give information and description of the marks at every police office. Well, the cup was found in an iron safe at this

Gralli's, and there was a lot of dollars in the safe with it. Well, the man that found the cup had just been having his lesson about the marked money ; and having his head full of it, thought he would have a look at this Signor Gralli's money, seeing that he seemed a looseish sort of fish. And sure enough among the dollars he found those two. So they sent for Signor Gralli at Florence, and asked him to have the goodness to say where he got those two dollars. Luckily he was able to say that he took them from the men who sold him the cup in change out of the gold pieces in which he paid for it. And a slight turn of the screw brought out the names and whereabouts of our friend Signor Michele and his comrade. Our fellows were down upon them an hour or two afterwards, and found almost all the rest of the marked dollars! The other fellow, Pasqualuccio as they call him, would not say a word. But our friend Michele is a clever rascal, and knows which side his own bread is buttered. He very soon made his own terms with the Procuratore Generale, and made a clean breast of it. There's the story of it; and I am heartily glad that it has turned out so for your sake, Signor Caroli!"

"Stefano Gralli!" said Carlo. "Why, that's the name of the man who . . . I had occasion to mention the name of Stefano Gralli to the Signor Commissario at Pescia, with reference to another matter I had to trouble him with, and I observed that he seemed struck with the name."

"Yes! because he had had the report of the cup stolen in his district having been found in Gralli's shop. I have heard something about that other affair you allude to, Signor Caroli; and no doubt you will soon hear something more of it. However, I will not meddle with business that has not come under my jurisdiction. I will only say that I wish the affairs of everybody who has to do with us had as pleasant an ending as yours are likely to have. Allow me once again," added the Commissario, taking Carlo's hand, "to congratulate you very sincerely on going out of this place thoroughly cleared from every shade of suspicion in that Sponda Lunga matter."

Carlo thanked him, and left the office together with Morini, feeling as if he was walking on air.

"It will be a great pleasure to me, Signor Caroli," said the lawyer, "to give this good news to our friends at home!"

"Thanks, Signor Morini!" said Carlo. "But if you will permit me to accompany you to your door, I think I should prefer doing that myself."

CHAPTER V

DURING the short walk from the police-office to the lawyer's house, nothing could exceed the efforts of Signor Morini to be civil, and to make himself agreeable to Carlo Caroli. It was not that Signor Giacomo had any great affection for the young manager of his old client the Signora Marta Monaldi's thriving business. It would probably be doing the lawyer no wrong to assert that he also, as well as his son, would have been well pleased if it had so turned out that Carlo had been indeed guilty of stealing the widow's money, and had disappeared from the world of Lucca, Sponda Lunga, and Ripalta accordingly. But Signor Giacomo Morini was not a hater of the calibre of Andrea Simonetti, nor was he

a man at all disposed to let likings or dis-
likings interfere with the steady and judicious
pursuit of his own interests.

He had become pretty well convinced that it
was all over with the hope of seeing his son
become the husband of Regina and the farmer's
heir. And he bitterly upbraided his son with
the folly and imprudence which had destroyed
so fair a prospect. He had tried very hard
to remedy the mischief which Meo's precipitate
desire to enjoy the ruin of his rival had caused.
But he had found the attempt hopeless. He
had known all along, far better than his son, that
the will of the lady herself was strong against
his hopes. But the will of young ladies on
such subjects, in the times and places with
which Signor Morini was conversant, was not
so frequently permitted to interfere with the
plans of their elders, as to induce him to consider this a very important obstacle. As long
as the will of Bartoli himself stood firm in
favour of the alliance, the lawyer doubted not
that it would in time be brought about. But
now he hoped no longer. The way in which

the farmer met his attempts at healing the
wound his son had made convinced him that
it was a lost game. He knew the farmer well;
and he recognised the fact that though Regina's
wishes might have been overborne by her
father's authority, yet that in the new position
of matters they were a strong additional force
against him.

But it did not follow that he was to lose
so valuable and influential a client as the
farmer! It was necessary to accept what
could not be helped with a good grace. And
he thought he saw too very well how things
were going. He had not been at all afraid
that the farmer's strongly expressed feeling of
gratitude towards Caroli for the service rendered to his daughter, or his consequent liking
for the young man, would lead Bartoli to the
length of consenting to give Regina's hand to
a penniless suitor. Still less was it to be supposed that he would consent to any such connection with a man on whose name such a
cloud rested, as that which had come over
Caroli. But now matters were changed, and

seemed likely to change more. Regina had not failed to tell her father the story of the prize in the lottery before he had heard anything of it from Carlo himself, and he had repeated it to the lawyer. Morini's lawyer-like sharpness led him to form a very strong opinion from the facts told to him that the priest of Uzzano had in some way or other possessed himself of the money ; and he was disposed to think that it would be recovered. He had noted the word or two that had dropped from the Commissary on this subject, and had observed the tone and manner in which they had been spoken. And he was thence led more strongly to the persuasion that the important sum in question was in a fair way of being restored to its legitimate owner.

In a word, the star of Signor Carlo Caroli was rising into the ascendant ; and the prudent lawyer made haste to worship accordingly.

And Carlo, though he did not kindly cotton to the man, had no reason to be angry with him. He was happy—ah ! so happy !—and disposed, therefore, as all men except the very bad are disposed, when they are happy, to be kindly and good-humoured to all around them.

" I daresay you don't know now, Signor Carlo "—the lawyer began after he had offered his own congratulations—" I dare say now you don't know how many people will be delighted at the result of this morning's business! To think of that wretched young man! Who ever heard of such wickedness! Ha! I see now plain enough how it was that my poor Meo was led into believing you to be guilty. It was the influence of that infamous scoundrel. I wish Meo had never seen so much of him! But *che vuole?* In business one is led to make the acquaintances that one's business leads to! How I pity his father!"

" It can't be denied, Signor Morini, that appearances were horribly against me! There is no telling how much I have suffered under it! Nevertheless, there were some people," said Carlo proudly, " who would not believe me to be guilty of theft despite all the appearances."

" Of course there were! *A chi lo dite!*

Why you don't suppose that *I* imagined you to have been guilty ! Pooh—pooh ! But I confess that I did not see any clear and comfortable way out of the position."

"It is a very great mercy—a matter to be very thankful for," said Carlo with a serious air, "that circumstances have turned out as they have ! Do you think I shall find Signor Bartoli at home ?"

"I don't know ! I hardly think you will ! He talked of going over to Ripalta this morning. That is a very curious story of your poor mother's lottery ticket, Signor Carlo ! You will excuse my mentioning it. But it seems to me that you may be in need of some professional assistance in the matter, and it is permissible, you know, for a man to offer the wares he deals in !" said the lawyer, with a smile ; " if you *should* need any advice or help of any kind, you may depend on my giving the matter my best attention. No offence !"

" *Che ! Anzi !* Signor Morini. But the truth is that I have been so beat down by this other matter, and my mind has been so full of it, that

I have hardly given any serious thought to the lottery ticket. It is, as you say, a very strange story.
I suppose you heard all about it from Bartoli."

"Yes! and from what he says, as far as I
can make out, I have little doubt that the
priest up there at Uzzano has got the money.
And my opinion is that with a little activity
and judicious management, the money might
be recovered. It will need delicate handling
though! Suppose that he admits that he has
it, and says that your mother made it over to
him for pious uses ? "

"What, ten thousand crowns ! " said Carlo.

"Yes, I know. It is a very large sum;
and I do not say that eventually the tribunals
would allow him to keep it. Under all the
circumstances probably not. But gifts as preposterous—forgive me for saying so !—have
been made, and have been held good! It
would not be all plain sailing ! It would be
a long and costly and thorny litigation. The
matter requires delicate handling, as I said—
very delicate handling indeed ! "

"Well ! we shall see what the Commissary

at Pescia has to say to me about it; for this other Commissary here seemed to say that I should soon hear from him on the subject. Now we shall see if Signor Giovanni is home!" added Carlo, as they reached the door of the lawyer's house.

"If he is not—if he is gone to Ripalta, as I take it he is," returned the lawyer, with a look that was meant to be exceedingly arch and confidential, "I dare say there may be somebody here that you are perhaps equally in a hurry to tell your news to! No doubt you will find the Signorina Regina at home!"

Carlo was considerably at a loss to understand the spirit in which the lawyer's last words had been spoken. Was it a good or an evil augury for his hopes? Had the lawyer abandoned the idea of a marriage between Regina and his son? Had the farmer spoken words which convinced him that he really wished to see a marriage between his daughter and himself? At all events it was a question to be discussed between him and Regina. And eager as he was to tell Signor Bartoli the result of his visit to the Commissary, he could not help feeling that it would be better still to tell it first to Regina in the presence of no third person.

So he simply said, "Yes! If the farmer is out, I shall be very glad if I can see the Signorina Regina. I should like to tell her what I have to tell."

Farmer Bartoli had gone to Ripalta, they found; and the lawyer went into his studio, telling Caroli that he might go up-stairs and find Regina. Carlo bounded up the steps, and almost ran over the Signora Morini as she was just coming out of the sitting-room on to the landing place.

"*Misericordia!* Signor Caroli! Is that you? *Santa Maria!* what a hurry you are in! Well, I suppose, I can guess who it is you are in such a hurry to see! It is not me; so I will go into the kitchen, as I was just a going when you ran up the stairs. Is Morini come in, do you know? You will find the Signorina Regina in the *Salottino*."

"Thanks, signora. Yes, Signor Morini has

just come in," said Carlo, passing to the door of the *Salottino*. " What, the wife too in the same story ! " he thought to himself as he entered the room. " Surely they must all . . . ."

But his thought had time to shape itself into no further words, There was Regina sitting by the window at the further end of the little room, and all alone ! She sprang from her chair as he entered, and came running towards him with outstretched arms.

" What news ! what news ! " she cried ; " say in one word, good news or bad ? "

" Good news!—very good news ! my own dear love ! " he answered, catching her in his arms and straining her to his bosom as he spoke the words, while her face, uplifted towards his, changed from pale to a brilliant rosy flush, and faded back again to white with the violence of her emotion.

" Is it . . . . is all right ? " she said, her lips parted with eagerness, and her eyes widely opened to devour the expression of his face.

" It is—for me—all right! There is no further question, my Regina, of my having touched this money!" said Carlo, still holding her in his arms, and looking down into her face with tender seriousness.

"Oh, thank God! thank God!" she said, raising herself a little on tiptoe as she spoke, so as to bring her lips a little nearer to his face. He bent his towards them, and their lips met for the first time in a long, lingering kiss.

"Let me sit down, my Carlo, I am so happy!" she said, bursting into violent tears, as he allowed her to sink on to a chair, while he leaned over her. "I am so happy! I am so happy! I am so happy!" she continued to repeat amid hysterical sobs.

Italian country girls are not apt to be hysterical; and Regina, healthy and vigorous in mind and body, was as little liable to such a weakness as any one among them. But she had suffered much during the past days—very much more than she had allowed to be visible to anybody. While she had given Carlo the comfort and support of unfaltering, buoyant hopefulness, she had in secret suffered fully as acutely as he had suffered from the cruel position in which he had been placed. And now the reaction was too much for her. She kept his hand convulsively clasped in hers, and drawing it down to her pressed it against her bosom, as if it had possessed a healing virtue.

"I am sure I don't know why I cry, *Carlo mio!*" she said, when she had become a little calmer; "for I am very happy!—and oh, so thankful! But somehow I cannot help it. I did not cry in all those past days. And now it seems as if I was crying the tears for the sorrow that has gone past. It is very silly, isn't it? . . . . . But I won't cry any more! . . . . Aren't you happy, Carlo? *Aren't* you? Oh, my love! . . . . my own love! . . . . you guilty of being a thief!" And then she burst out again into a fresh passion of tears. But they were sweet, not bitter tears. And Carlo soon succeeded in calming her.

Then he told all the extraordinary story that had come to his knowledge that morning. And the astonishment and indignation of Regina at Simonetti's crime were so great that it was difficult to say which sentiment was the

strongest. It was with simple truth that she
said she could not have believed such baseness
and wickedness to be possible. It opened to
her a new and terrible vista into the capabili-
ties of her fellow-creatures for abasement! And
that this viper should have power so to sting
her own treasure—her beloved—the noble upright heart that was incapable of conceiving
such infamy!

But then came softer and happier thoughts;
—of sorrows, and doubts, and difficulties past—
of happiness to come!

Oh, yes! Regina understood the behaviour of
Signor and Signora Morini well enough, as she
admitted with a laughing blush, so delicious to
the sight that Carlo could not refrain from trying
the taste of it also. But this time he was not
permitted to be as long about the operation as in
that first moment of delight that told her that
the sorrow which abideth for a night had passed
away, and that the joy which cometh with the
morning had arrived.

"Now, Carlo, that is enough . . . . for the
present. We are here to talk—*niente altro*.—

please to observe, and I shall never be able to understand all you have to tell me, if you go on in that way. Yes, Signor Giacomo and Signora Maria, they understand which way the wind is blowing. And it is a very good sign. Signor Giacomo knows father well—better, perhaps, than anybody else. You may depend upon it, father has said enough to him to let him know that . . . that . . . that it is to be all right," she said, completing her sentence with another rosy blush.

And then they discussed the ten thousand dollar question, and the probabilities of the recovery of the money; by no means disguising from themselves, or from each other, the fact that this point might count for much in the speedy realisation of their wishes.

"But father has a great opinion of Signor Giacomo's cleverness," said Regina; "and if he thinks that you will get the money, father will feel very sure that you will."

"But whether I do or don't, my own love, *anima mia,* however it may turn out, that will make no difference between us, and . . . ."

" Of course, not in the end ! . . . . but father
. . . . I would tell father all at once, Carlo, and
say that whether the money comes or not . . . .
For father . . . ."

But here the two heads which were very
literally being laid together on this knotty
point, were quickly drawn to a greater distance
from each other, and the owners of them
assumed that specially foolish appearance which
people are apt to assume when suddenly interrupted in such converse. For the door of the
Salottino was hurriedly opened, and the farmer
himself entered.

CHAPTER VI.

A BARGAIN.

It was evident at once on the farmer's entry into the room that he was by no means displeased at finding Carlo there. He came forward smilingly, with extended hands.

"What Carlo, my boy!" Carlo could not help smiling at finding himself promoted to that form of salutation, *vice* Meo Morini superseded. "What, Carlo, my boy, you here? Glad to see you! Any news?"

"News indeed, father! Such news!" cried Regina, with a beam in her eye, and a smile on her lip that might have been a cure for many sorrows to look on. "Signor Carlo stands righted before the world! The robbery at the widow's house is all found out!"

"No! you don't say so! But I knew it

would be so. Signor Carlo, I congratulate you
with all my heart. Not that I had any doubt
about it at all, as you know. But, then, I am
not all the world."

"But, father," said Regina, with a serious
look, "you would never guess,—nobody would
ever guess, who the guilty person is—at least,
the most guilty ! "

" Why, you don't mean to say that it was anybody 1 know ? " said the farmer, with a look
almost of alarm.

Regina nodded gravely once or twice.

" What ! not . . . . " and the farmer gave a
glance with his eyes, and made a little movement with his thumb, which said very plainly,
"anybody in this house ?—not . . . . not Meo
Morini ? "

" Oh, no! no ! no ! " said Regina and Carlo
in chorus. " No ! Signor Meo is not so bad as
all that comes to," added Carlo.

" Well, then, I wish I may be shot if I can
guess who you mean. Who was it ? " he asked
in the low tones of one who speaks about something too terrible to be generally talked about.

Carlo looked at Regina.

"Tell father," she said; "tell him all about it."

The farmer looked with wondering eyes from one to the other of them.

"It was Signor Andrea Simonetti, who put up two regular thieves—housebreakers from Leghorn—to steal the money," said Carlo, in a low and grave voice.

"*Misericordia!* Andrea Simonetti! *Dio di Dio!* Andrea Simonetti! Has he confessed that it was he who did it?"

"No, Signor Giovanni. He stands to it that he knows nothing about it. But one of the men who committed the robbery has confessed everything," said Carlo;—"and Simonetti is arrested," he added.

"*Dio di Dio! Dio di Dio!*" exclaimed the farmer again. "Why .... why, the fellow was not that hard pressed for money that he should think to do such a thing!"

"No. And he never touched a soldo of the money," said Carlo. "But he was present when the dollars were put away; he managed to get an impression of the key, and so helped these fellows to commit the robbery."

"And what for, in the name of all the saints, if he did not have any part of the money?" asked the farmer, with wide eyes.

"He did it from pure hatred of Carlo," said Regina, blushing as she became aware that in her eagerness she had omitted to put in the "Signor," as conventional etiquette required . . . . "because he wanted the suspicion of the robbery to rest on him."

"Well, I never heard of such a thing! But what do you know about it, my girl?" said the farmer.

"Only that Signor Carlo has just been telling me all about it; how it all came out before the Signor Commissario," said Regina, blushing again.

"But did he say he did it because he hated you, then?" asked the farmer, turning to Carlo.

"No, Signor Giovanni; he said nothing, except that it was all lies from beginning to end. But the man who confessed, told how he had asked Signor Simonetti what his interest in the robbery was, and he had answered, that he wished it done in order to ruin me," replied Carlo.

"Well! . . . . Well! . . . . Well! I never heard such a thing! I could not have imagined such a thing. *Santa Madonna!* And he is arrested, you say. And old Simonetti? *Dio mio! Dio mio!* And he has money of mine in his hands . . . the old man has. I shall tell Morini to get it in at once. *Misericordia! che cosa! che cosa!*" said the farmer, quite overwhelmed with astonishment. "Do you know," he added after a little pause, "whether any of the widow's money has been recovered? Morini tells me that it was all marked, and that he can swear to the dollars."

"I believe a considerable part of the sum has been found in the house of the fellows who committed the robbery," said Carlo.

"That's well, so far! . . . . I wish all your ten thousand dollars had been marked, Signor Carlo," said the farmer, musing.

"Yes, indeed, Signor Giovanni, I wish they

had. However, Signor Morini thinks that the sum will be recovered," said Carlo.

"Does he ?   Does Morini think so ?" said the farmer, earnestly.

"So he says," replied Carlo; "he told me so just now, and wanted to undertake the management of the business himself."

"Did he, though !" returned the farmer, "that is a very good sign—a *very* good sign ! Morini is a very sharp fellow. I never knew him wrong in a matter of this kind.   Well," he added suddenly, after a pause of some little duration, "and if the money is recovered, what then ?"

"Why, then," said Carlo, looking rather surprised, "then I shall come into possession of it."

"Of course you will. Nobody doubts that. That was not what I was thinking of.   But when you do come into possession of it, what do you mean to do ?" said the farmer, with a look at Carlo from under his eye-brows.

Carlo looked at him for an instant with a sharp, inquiring glance, and then his eyes met those of Regina. They spoke together an instant, with an interchange of thought far swifter than words ; and then Carlo replied, with desperate suddenness, to the farmer's question.

"The first thing I should do, Signor Giovanni, would be to ask your permission to seek your daughter for my wife!" said he.

Regina had known what was coming. But she had hardly realised the force of the shock the words, thus direct and naked, were calculated to produce ; and she turned away sharply to the window, with her chin well down upon her bosom, as if she had received a douche of cold water in her face.

"Well! that is speaking out!" said the farmer. "Well," he continued, slowly, "I don't see why you should not. But for you I should like enough have had never a daughter at all ; . . . . and ten thousand dollars is a very pretty bit of money . . . . a *very* pretty bit of money! So you don't mean to have anything to say to the widow, Signor Carlo?" he added, in a tone that seemed half banter, half earnest.

"Signor Giovanni! I am talking in earnest—not joking! Let us leave joking for another time, if you please."

"Well, but without any joking, you don't mean that you never did think of her?" said the farmer.

"I do mean to say in all seriousness that I never thought of such a thing for an instant. The Signora Marta has been good and kind to me in every way; and it would ill become me to hear such things said without giving them the most complete contradiction."

"Yet the widow is a very pretty woman—a charming woman—and the business must be a very good one!" said the farmer.

"All very true, Signor Giovanni," said Carlo, smiling; "but for all that, what I have told you is quite as true."

"What should you say, now, judging from the experience you have had, that the business turns in, net income, in the year?" asked Bartoli.

"Well!" said Carlo, not a little surprised at the line the farmer's thoughts seemed taking at a moment when he had invited them to move in so different a direction. " Well! I should say that the wheelwright business must net something like fifteen hundred dollars a year."

" Ay! so I should suppose! That is about what I should put it at!" said the farmer musingly. " And then," he added, " the widow has a pretty penny put by ! "

" I dare say she has !" said Carlo ; " but, Signor Giovanni, I was speaking to you on another subject,—and a more important one to me."

" To be sure, my boy ! to be sure ! Every man for himself. I am thinking of myself. I should be very lonely if you were to take my girl away from me ! Don't you see ? Very lonely ! And then as for Regina ! The last time there was any talk of marrying she swore she would not marry at all ;—would live an old maid ;—and go and be a nun, *e che so io !*—and I know not what all !" said the farmer.

" But you did not approve of that, father ! "

said Regina, half turning herself round from the window and speaking over her shoulder.

"No I didn't! So now you have thought better of it, eh! and mean to be an obedient daughter, and marry the man I bid you, eh?"

"If you give your consent, father . . . ." whispered Regina, quitting her place by the window, and coming close up to his side, and hanging her head lower than ever.

"If I bid you marry the man you have a mind to, you'll be as obedient a girl as any in Christendom! That's about it, isn't it, my girl?" said the farmer, but not ill-humouredly.

Regina nestled closer up to his side, and half hid her face on his shoulder. The farmer threw his arm loosely round her.

"To think of that infamous scoundrel, young Simonetti!" said the farmer, whose thoughts seemed to be singularly discursive that afternoon; "I wonder what the widow will think of it! People did use to say, at one time, that the Signora Marta had a liking for him."

"People say all sorts of lies and nonsense!" said Carlo; "I think I can say that no such thought ever entered into the widow's head! *Che!* the Signora Monaldi marry Andrea Simonetti!"

"You think she never cared for him at all?" asked the farmer.

"Not she," said Carlo; "why the Signora Monaldi is a thoroughly good woman, and a sensible woman too in her way. And you may trust me she knows what is what a deal too well ever to have given Signor Simonetti a thought!"

"How old a woman is the widow?" asked the farmer, who seemed to Carlo willing to talk upon any subject save the, to him, all important one he was waiting for an answer upon.

"Really I can't say for certain!" returned Carlo; "but I should say, about thirty-five;—somewhere thereabouts!"

"Thirty-five!" said the farmer thoughtfully; —"thirty-five!—a very good age!—a very good age! . . . . and a very good business!

. . . . and a very handsome woman! Certainly a very handsome woman ! . . . . Fifteen hundred dollars a year ! Yes! that will be about it ! That will be about the mark ! "

Regina had continued all this time closely nestled up to her father's side, but glancing at Carlo from time to time as the farmer spoke, with a look of surprised inquiry. Suddenly, after a silence of a minute or two, the farmer changed his attitude with a start so violent as almost to throw her off from him, and striking his hand flat on the table near which he had been standing, after the manner of a man striking a bargain, said :

" Look here, Caroli, my boy, this is what it is ! If I give you my girl, and marry the widow myself, will you continue to manage the business at Sponda Lunga ? That's all about it ! "

Carlo and Regina involuntarily looked at each other in amazement. Not that there was anything very absurd or preposterous in the farmer's proposal,—but that it was so utterly new, and so unexpectedly propounded to them.

The farmer's age might be about fifty-five; and he was a perfectly hale, hearty, and active man. But he had been a widower now for nearly five years; and although people had said when he first became so, that Farmer Bartoli would of course marry again, for some time past it had come to be considered as much out of the question that he should do so, as that the Archbishop of Lucca should take a wife.

"Well!" said the farmer, after waiting a moment or two. "Well! is it a bargain? What do you say? Will you have my girl upon those terms?"

"Of course I will, Signor Giovanni," said Carlo with a smiling shrug; "of course I am only too happy to agree to those or pretty well any other terms you could propose to me,— but . . . . it seems to me that, even if I am so happy as to count on the consent of the Signorina Regina, there is another person who ought to be consulted on the subject."

"Another person! another person to be consulted about marrying Regina! What other person?" asked the farmer indignantly.

"No other person certainly, Signor Giovanni, about the marriage of the Signorina Regina. On that subject I want no other word than your consent and hers. But as to the condition that you proposed . . . it seems that we cannot consider anything settled till Signora Marta has been consulted!" said Carlo, with some approach to a smile.

"Ah, the widow! What, whether she'll have me, you mean! Ah! I see! I see! Well, you see, Carlo, my boy, girls are girls, and widows are widows. · You do your wooing, and win your own wife; and leave me to do mine! Is it all right if the widow becomes my wife? You will marry Regina, and continue to act as manager of the business at Sponda Lunga? Is *that* all right?" said the farmer.

Carlo stepped up to Regina, who had returned to her place at the window, and taking her hand, while placing himself so as to be between the farmer and his daughter, said, as he bent his head till his lips lightly touched her forehead, "May I say yes! to your father's proposal, *anima mia?* Will you be my wife, my own only love ?"

"I said it that terrible night, Carlo, at the door of the widow's house! I never meant then to change. I never shall and never can change. I was yours then, yours ever since. and yours ever more, Carlo, *my* Carlo !"

She hung her head and spoke so low that her voice could not reach her father. But her lover heard and treasured each precious word.

"Well! have you made up your minds yet?" said the farmer. "You seem to be a long time about it !"

"We had done it some time ago, I think, signore ! But we had to consult about the conditions, you know ! " said Carlo, looking while he spoke into Regina's face.

"Ah, whether she would be content to go and live in the widow's house at Sponda Lunga ?"

"I like that house better than any other in all the world ! " said Regina, looking not at her father, but shyly into her lover's face.

"So, then it is all settled ! Very good !

Now I shall go to Sponda Lunga and settle my part of the affair. I shall be back by supper time."

And so saying the farmer left the room, and the happy lovers heard him the next minute leave the house.

CHAPTER VII.

SIGNOR GIOVANNI PROPOSES.

FARMER BARTOLI left the room and the house to get into a *bagarino* for his short drive to Sponda Lunga on the errand he had stated himself to be about to undertake, and left Carlo and Regina together. Which party shall we follow? The generality of readers, it seems reasonable to suppose, will be more able to imagine for themselves what passed between the two latter personages, than to follow in their fancies the proceedings of the former. We will, therefore, leave the lovers to themselves, and hang on behind the farmer's *bagarino* and fast trotting pony, as he bowled along the level road to the widow's house on the banks of the Serchio.

Carlo and Regina had several good hours

before them—all the hours intervening between
four o'clock, or thereabouts, and supper-time, in
the lawyer's house. And they felt tolerably
sure that they should not be disturbed till
old Aurora came to prepare the table in the
salottino for that meal. The male members of
the family, when they once descended to the
studio after dinner, rarely came up-stairs again
till they were called to supper. And the Signora Morini was wont to pass those afternoon
hours—unless it was a *festa*—between her
kitchen and own room. So that the lovers
had the room to themselves and the happy
hours before them. They did not exactly
"dream the happy hours away." Happiness
was as yet too new for that—too imperfectly
surveyed, realised, and examined in every part
of it. They had so much to think of—so much
to talk about! Yet, it was not all talk that
passed between them.

But there ! *Virginibus puerisque canto !* In
a canto, you understand, my dear madam, intended for the lads and lasses, can it be necessary to enlarge on these matters, or to play the

spy on such a *téte-à-téte?* They know all about it! And we will be off with the farmer on his way to his less-stereotyped courtship.

The farmer was a man rarely troubled with misgivings in any of the affairs of life. His own view of the matter was that a man with such a balance at his banker's as he had, could have no business with misgivings. And though innate temperament has, of course, the main share of influence in such matters, there are many men proud of their self-confidence and bold energy, who owe a larger portion of these good gifts to the circumstance to which Farmer Bartoli attributed them in his own case, than they are aware of. The farmer, I say, was not a man liable to misgivings ; and he was .troubled with none on the present occasion.

A personable man was Farmer Bartoli ! There would have been more of the general effect of the Apollo Belvidere about him, per- haps, had his longitudinal measurement been somewhat greater in proportion to his lati- tudinal, than was the case. It had been so once. But for the last seven lustres the former had been stationary, while the latter had slowly but unceasingly increased. Nectar and ambrosia, it may be presumed, do not operate towards any such result; but a long course of maccaroni and Chianti unquestionably does. The broad, smiling, sun-browned features of his face were decidedly good. The brow was not high; but it was fairly broad. He had a bright black eye under a huge shaggy brow, that could still flash on due occasion; a straight nose; a clear, deep, ruddy, brown complexion that was a sure guarantee of health and soundness to the core; a clean shaved chin; a short upper lip, also cleanly shaven; and a large mouth, whose broad frank smile, showing a range of faultless white teeth, was really handsome. A black low-crowned round hat, with a stiff brim fully three inches wide, was on his head. He sat, as he drove, square and solid in the middle of the low backless seat of the little *bagarino*, leaving on either side of the broad extent of black velveteen jacket which clothed his back and shoulders, so small a vacant space as to indicate that none but a companion of very different

mould could have dreamed of sharing his con-
veyance with him. The front view of him as
he sat thus, nearly filling the little carriage, presented an equally broad expanse of scarlet, dot-
ted over with mother-of-pearl buttons. He had
a pair of dark-coloured breeches of coarse
woollen cloth, tied with ribbons very close
beneath the knee ; and two stalwart legs
clothed in light blue worsted stockings and
thick low-cut shoes, reposed almost at their full
length on the low floor of the *bagarino* in front
of him. It was a smart-looking little carriage,
the unpainted wood of which was highly var-
nished, of its own natural colour. The reins
were of round red worsted cords, almost as
large as the bell-ropes in a belfry ; the harness
was lavishly ornamented with plated metal ;
there was a collar of small not altogether un-
musically jingling bells around the pony's neck,
and two long red feathers standing upright on
either side of his head.

No part of the farmer's array had been
assumed with any special reference to his present errand. For, as has been seen, he had

started on it suddenly and unpremeditatedly. His sojourn in the city had perhaps caused the costume, which at Ripalta would have been appropriated to *festa* days, to be used *en permanence*. And the farmer had not conceived it necessary to make the smallest alteration in it with a view to the business he had in hand.

The widow Monaldi was sitting in an easy chair in her little parlour; and having no trouble or care to keep her awake, she was fast asleep—a sleep more placid, but only slightly so, than the tranquil serenity of her waking hours. But Assunta, her old maid, having more cares upon her mind in reference to the *governaré*-ing of the utensils which had been used for her mistress's dinner, and subsequently for her own—the washing-up, in more homely English—Assunta was awake. And she heard the jingling of the farmer's horse-bells as the *bagarino* passed the front of the cottage, and in accordance with the habitudes of the place, passed on to the entrance of the work-yard, so as to drive up to the back door, which opened on it. A half glance from her kitchen window

sufficed to tell Assunta who was the visitor;
and like an invaluable factotum as she was, she
rushed into the parlour to warn her mistress of
the farmer's approach, before opening the door
to him.

" Keep him at the door a minute, Sunta ! "
cried the widow, fully herself in an instant.

No one acquainted only with the usual soft
languid placidity of the Signora Marta's move-
ments on ordinary occasions would have guessed
that it was possible for her to move so alertly as
she stepped across the room to the pier glass
which was hanging between the two windows.
There in an instant the snow-white cap was
adjusted just a thought more jauntily on the
glossy raven-black head than it had been before,
and the satiny braids of hair which it left visible
were smoothed over the milk-white brow which
they encircled. A moistened finger was rapidly
but with dexterous precision passed over each
dark admirably-arched eyebrow. The soft lovely
eyes needed no supervision of any kind. They
were always ready for the most active service on
the shortest possible notice. The white crape

neck-kerchief was skilfully and judiciously ar-
ranged—not, however, with the single unerring
touch which had sufficed for the other small
matters which have been mentioned. The
snowy folds, less pure in tint than the swelling
bosom and rounded shoulders, which they
partly hid and partly gave to sight, were pulled
down and back a bit, and then pulled forward a
thought more across the bosom.

It would be a mistake to imagine that all
these little cares were prompted by any special
desire on the part of the widow to captivate
the farmer. Not a bit of it! She would have
done exactly the same had she expected the
visit of any one of the sons of Adam—as
distinguished from his daughters. It was a
sort of natural quit-rent due in recognition of
homage to be paid to the suzerain sex, which the
widow's principles never allowed her to neglect.

Having prepared herself for the due perform-
ance of this duty, she turned towards the door
with a gentle smile of suave welcome on her
prettily-curved lip, and the farmer entered.

"Signor Giovanni, of all people in the world!

Why you are quite a stranger in this part of the world since you have been in Lucca!"

"Yes, I am, more's the pity, Signora Marta! I am heartily tired of it, I can tell you!"

"Do you come from Ripalta now, Signor Giovanni? Is there any matter wanted in our line?" said the widow, with a killing *œillade*.

"No! I have driven over from Lucca straight here. And I came on purpose to pay a visit to you, Signora Marta!" said the farmer, with a business-like directness of manner and tone.

"That is very kind! I take it very kind, Signor Giovanni!" with a glance that would have burned a hole in a deal board. "How is the Signorina Regina? None the worse, I hope, for what she went through that dreadful night."

"Not a bit! No! She is all the better for that night, *she* is!"

The widow opened her large eyes still wider in surprise; but the farmer went on with what he wanted to say, unheeding her wonder.

"Yes, signora, I came out on purpose to see

you, because I have something I want to say to you; but it is not about anything in the wheelwright line."

"Indeed, Signor Giovanni! Well, I am glad it is not about anything to do with the business. For I do not think Signor Carlo is at home. And it is little I know about it myself."

"No! I know Caroli is not at home, because I left him at Lucca. And talking of him brings me part way to what I come here to say. First of all, you'll be glad to hear that he is quite clear out of all the affair about the robbery here!"

"That's good news, indeed, Signor Giovanni! I am very glad, for the poor fellow fretted about it so. Not that I ever dreamed that he knew anything about the money! Lord bless you! But those lawyer chaps are so bothering! But what's been found out about it?"

And then the farmer told in a succinct straightforward manner all the story of the concoction of the robbery by Simonetti, and the manner in which it had been found out.

Of course the widow's astonishment, indignation, commiseration, and final rejoicing kept due pace with the progress of the farmer's narrative.

"But why did that wicked good-for-nothing wretch hate poor Signor Caroli to such an awful degree ? That is what I cannot understand !" said the widow, dropping her fine eyes demurely on to her lap beneath their long silken lashes, and folding her plump white hands before her.

The farmer looked at her with a shrewd half-laughing glance out of the corner of his eye, as he said, in reply—

"Ay ! That's what I say ! Why—what for —what harm had he ever done to Simonetti? It looks almost like jealousy. When there's a woman in the case, and a man is jealous, he will do anything. But I don't see how there could be any room for jealousy. It's true my girl always did listen to Carlo in a way she would never listen to anyone else. But what was that to Simonetti? He never dared to look at Regina in that way. I should think not, indeed ! "

"But I thought that the Signora Regina was, as one might almost say, engaged to Signor Meo Morini?" said the widow, folding and unfolding her pretty white hands in a slightly nervous manner, which with her was equivalent to another person's bounding and jumping on their chair.

"*Che! Che!* not at all! Engaged! Not a bit of it! Regina would never look at him. I wanted it—the more fool I! The girl knew better! But I found out what Signor Meo was in this last business of the robbery. Why what do you think he did that day when it was found out here? Goes back to Lucca as fast as he can lay leg to ground, and goes to the police, telling 'em all about it, and setting 'em on, and making 'em believe that he was sent by you to fetch 'em! And then he comes to me as pleased as Punch to tell me that Signor Carlo was found out to be a thief, and was to go to the galleys, just for all the world as if it was the best news in the world, and came like cheese on the maccaroni. I never was so disgusted with a man in my life. I pretty

soon told him that *he* was not the sort of stuff
I wanted for a son-in-law! Son-in-law! Yes!
that is just the word for it. He wanted to be
son-in-law to the farmer at Ripalta! I don't
believe he cared a bit for Regina! Now this
other fellow—your cousin, is he not, Signora
Marta?—I believe him when he says he has
never had eyes nor ears for any other woman
since he first saw her! And a very handsome
couple they will make! Won't they, Signora
Marta?"

"Is it settled then that it is to be a match,
Signor Bartoli? I must say I do think Signor
Caroli might have told me the news himself!"
said the widow, still with her eyes fixed on her
hands, which were lying in her lap before her.

"No doubt he will tell you himself, Signora
Marta! and no doubt he would have been the
first to tell you the news if I had not been
before-hand with him. But it was only settled
an hour ago; and I left him with Regina, and
came straight over here to see you!" said the
farmer, looking hard at her, and intending probably to look tenderly.

"Come straight to see me!" repeated the
widow, with an air of being completely mystified. "I do not understand . . . I really . . .
What can I have to say to Signor Caroli's marriage? I am sure I wish him all happiness,
and . . . and . . . and . . . "

The gentle widow finished her sentence by
gently pressing the corner of her handkerchief
to her downcast eyes.

"Well, you see," continued the farmer, still
watching her closely, "that it is not quite, as a
body may say, settled for good and all. That
is, it is settled between them, as far as they can
settle it. But it is not quite settled that I give
my consent, for there was a condition I made
before giving it."

"Indeed, Signor Giovanni!" said the widow,
more and more mystified; "and if I may ask,
what was the condition? Was it something
that the young folks would not agree to, that
you left them without coming to a settle-
ment?"

"Well, you see, they were willing enough to
consent as far as it depended on them. But it

did not depend upon them altogether. It depended partly—mainly, I should say—upon another person," said the farmer, with Sibilline oracularness.

"Dear me! another person! But that seems rather hard upon them, if their hearts are made up to it, don't it, Signor Giovanni? Who is it that has any right to a word in the matter except yourself? As for poor Caroli, he has neither father nor mother, nor anybody else, the more's the pity. May I ask who the other person is?" said the widow, raising her eyes and looking for a wonder not languishingly, but simply inquiringly, at the farmer.

"That other person," said the farmer, getting up from his chair and stepping across to place himself immediately in front of the widow, and looking down into her face, as she looked up at him in wonder what was coming next, . . . "that other person, widow, is the Signora Marta Monaldi."

"*Santa Madonna!* Signor Giovanni! *me!*" cried the widow, while the whole fair expanse of white neck, cheek, and brow became sud-

denly suffused with a bright, delicate, rosy hue;
"why, what can I have to say in the matter?
Signor Caroli needs no consent of mine, I suppose ? "

"No! Signora Marta; Caroli is free to marry
whom he pleases, I suppose. But it was I, Signora Marta, that made a condition, which depended on you. And it depends on you so
entirely that before finally giving my consent
I came over hot foot to *you!*" said the farmer,
with a particular sort of emphasis, the widow
thought, on the word "you," and looking down
into her large eyes, in which he could see the
reflection of his own face.

A kind of half glimmer of a notion of the
farmer's real meaning shot like a swift-passing
phantom across the widow's brain, and caused
the large eyes to droop beneath his, and the
delicate rosy tint to return to the face and
brow.

"Really, Signor Giovanni," she said, "you
are talking riddles to me! I have not the least
idea what you mean. What can I do or say in
the matter either to make or to mar? How

does it concern me in any way? I have no
interest in the matter, I assure you!" she
added, driven into the woman's lie rather ex-
cusably, poor soul, by the hard lines meted out
to her.

"It is true, Signora Marta, that I was
thinking most of my own interest in the matter.
If Regina leaves me, I shall be a very lonely
man, Signora Marta!"

Then the widow almost felt certain that she
understood him! And her thought rushed with
the rapidity of a lightning flash over a compre-
hensive survey of the advantages and disad-
vantages, social, sentimental, and material, of
the position of her who should become Signora
Bartoli of Ripalta the second, while from beneath the covert of her long eye-lashes she
stole a passing but rapidly-critical glance at the
broad red expanse of the farmer's waistcoat, and
the broad red expanse of the farmer's good-
natured face.

It might be supposed that the widow would
have again replied to the farmer's remark, that
he should be a lonely man when his daughter

married, by reiterating her own demand for explanation, how it could in any way concern her,
or what she could have to do with the myste-
rious condition to which the farmer had alluded.
But she did not do this. She only raised her
eyes, half shyly veiled by their lashes, to his face,
and said, " La ! Signor Giovanni, do you think
so ? "

"Certainly, I think so. There can be no
doubt about it. In course I should. I should
be a lonely, miserable man," said the farmer;
". . . . unless . . . . unless "—and here he
stooped down and took one of the white, plump,
unresisting hands that were lying in the widow's
lap, and held it in his own broad, brown palm,
and so paused for a second or two ; then went
on suddenly, bending over her as he spoke,—
" Look here, Signora Marta, don't you trouble
yourself to say a word. If it is to be as I hope,
you sit still while I give you a kiss, as is right
and proper. If it is not to be, you bob your
head out of the way, and I shall know I have no
hope. Here goes ! "

And so saying, the farmer slowly and gra-

dually bent his head lower and lower, till his lips
all but touched the fair white forehead beneath
them.   He could see the light folds of the mus-
lin which lay on the widow's bosom rise and fall
with an unusual agitation, but the glossy black
head was not " bobbed away," and the symbolic
kiss was given and received.

" That's right !   Well done !   You've made
me a happy man," said the farmer ; "and, please
Heaven, I will make you a good husband, and
you shall never have cause to repent this day's
work ! "

" But it does seem very sudden, doesn't it,
dear Signor Giovanni ? " said the widow, looking
at him with all that love which for ever shone in
her eyes, and then bashfully dropping them.

" Good luck is never too sudden.   What's the
good of standing shilly shally about it,—keeping
those two others waiting too !   For I told 'em
my consent depended on your consent.   And
now we are right all round, and we will all be
married the same day."

" Why, what a man you are, farmer, for
doing things off-hand in a hurry ! " said the

widow. " You are for all the world just like a boy ! "

"And you look as coy about it, for all the world, as a young girl ! " said the farmer, with a great laugh.

" Don't you talk nonsense, farmer ! Silly boobies may be old as well as young!" retorted the widow.

And then there was a deal of talk of future plans and arrangements. Caroli was to manage the business, with a half share in it; and he and his wife were to live in the widow's house at Sponda Lunga. A new house was to be built in more modern fashion on the site of the old one at Ripalta; and the farmer, before he declared that he must go back to the couple at the lawyer's house, and tell them that the condition was accepted, had proved himself to be a truly enamoured man, by consenting that the parlour and best bed-room of the new house at Ripalta should be adorned by the unprecedented magnificence of paper hangings.

CHAPTER VIII.

THE FARMER TRIUMPHANT.

The farmer drove back to Lucca in a state of high good humour and considerable triumph and exultation. He considered that he had conducted the delicate transaction on which he had been engaged in a masterly and judicious manner, which did the highest credit to his talents for business, and his knowledge of mankind;—and specially his possession of that knowledge, of which gentlemen of his time of life are apt to be still more proud—his knowledge of womankind.

He sat in the middle of the seat of his little carriage, gave the good Maremma pony the rein, cracking his whip loudly from time to time, after the approved fashion of Italian coachmanship, while the little horse-bells jingled merrily, and

the late autumn sun was setting behind the low
hills that were between him and the western
sea. There was only one subject of anxious
thought that mingled itself with his pleasant
self-congratulations. He would have liked that
that matter of the ten thousand dollars should
have been somewhat more clearly brought to a
happy termination before affairs were considered
to be quite settled between Regina and Carlo.
He had good hope, however, that all would be
well in this respect ; and he thought that
on the whole he had done wisely in permitting
the matter to take the turn it had. Ten thousand dollars was a great sum ;—a vast sum, indeed, for one like Caroli, who had never had
a *soldo* to bless himself with before, to become
suddenly possessed of. It was a sum, the farmer
felt, enough to turn a man's head. And though
he had a high opinion of Caroli, there was no
knowing whether so great a change of fortune
might not make a changed man. And any way
—that is, any other way than the way things had
gone—there would have been trouble with
Regina ! Then the resolution which he had

been led to himself, and on which he had acted
with such happy promptitude, was certainly a
very fortunate and wise one! Yes, it was all
best as it was; and the farmer, as he drove
through the narrow, dark archway piercing the
fortified wall of the city, was content to hope
that the ten thousand dollar affair would come
to as good an ending as the rest.

In another minute or two he drove up to the
lawyer's door, and leaving to Lao, the lawyer's
pale-faced clerk, the highly acceptable task of
driving the *bagarino* through the streets to the
stables, he went up to the room in which he had
left Carlo and Regina, taking the steps three at a
time, almost as impetuously as Carlo himself
had done, when told he might go and tell the
news of his recognised innocence to his mistress.

It yet wanted an hour or so to the lawyer's
supper hour, and Carlo and Regina were still
busy in enjoying to the utmost the delight of
each minute of the hours that would never again
return for either of them. They were astonished
at the farmer's quick return.

"Why, I thought, Signor Giovanni, that you

had started to go to Sponda Lunga!" said
Carlo.

"What made you change your mind, father?"
asked Regina.

"How do you mean, change my mind?" said
the farmer, staring at her. "I haven't changed
my mind. I'm not so apt to change my mind.
Of course I went to Sponda Lunga."

"Why, you don't mean, Signor Giovanni, that
you have been to Sponda Lunga and back again
since you left the room?" said Carlo.

"I do mean to say so. To be sure I have!
been to Sponda Lunga and back again, and done
a stroke of work there into the bargain!" said
the farmer, who felt the astonishment of those he
had left at his quick return to be complimentary
to his own veni-vidi-vici style of operations.

"Well, father?" said Regina, with a look of
laughing inquiry at her father. She felt tolerably
certain from her father's manner, that his visit
had not been a disagreeable one.

"Well!" returned he; "you may consider
the condition on which I gave my consent to a
marriage between you two as fulfilled. It is all

right ! though Signor Carlo *did* think it
was a matter of such doubt till the other
person had been consulted. There, it is all
right !"

" Upon my word, *Signor Socero,*" said Carlo,
laughing as he for the first time, somewhat
in anticipation, gave the farmer the title of
father-in-law ; " upon my word, *Signor Socero,*
you do not let the grass grow under your
feet ! "

" What's the good ! " said the farmer, with a
conquering air ; " what use is it ? When a man
has that knowledge of women that he sees how
to take 'em, what is the good, I say, of standing
shilly shally ! I do not know how it is, but in
my day, we youngsters used to see no fun in
spending weeks and months over getting a girl's
' yes ' from her. But the world's different, I
suppose, now-a-days. Yes, I see ! You've got
Regina to say ' yes ' at last. But how long were
you about it ? "

Carlo smiled, and stole a glance at Regina,
who blushed and hung her head, not without a
sly, laughing glance out of the corner of her eye,

however, which it may be supposed expressed much the same commentary on her father's remarks that Carlo's franker smile did.

" How long were you about it, now, I say ? " continued the farmer in a high state of good-humour and self-complacency. " My way is different. But, then, I have some experience of these things. You could not believe your eyes, you young 'uns, when you saw me come back from Sponda Lunga, all settled and done in less than a couple of hours, journey out, journey back, courting and all ! But that's what comes of knowing how to set about it, you see! Women . . . . Lord bless you, I know what women are ! "

" Ah, Signor Giovanni," said Carlo, looking at Regina while speaking to the farmer, " if you could only have told me of your secret at the beginning, instead of the end, of my wooing, what a lot of awful hard work it might have saved me ! "

" It wouldn't have been the least bit of use in the world, father," said Regina, in the same tone. " It wouldn't have saved him an hour or a word. And I have a good mind to show him as much by making him begin all over again!"

Her father looked at her with a proud smile on his broad frank face. "I suppose, Signor Carlo, that the fact is, the lasses are as much changed as the lads are! Any way, I've reached the same point that you have, though I only started a couple of hours ago, as you know. I told the widow that we would be married all four of us on the same day."

"I'd lay a wager, father, that you'll go on calling her the widow after you're married," said Regina.

"Nay, I must teach my tongue better than that any way. She is a right-down, dear, good woman as ever breathed, the widow is! Here comes Aurora to lay the supper. I suppose you mean to be off, Signor Carlo? The widow will expect to be told all about your affairs by your own word of mouth. She said she thought you might have told her yourself. But I let her know that you had nothing to tell till this afternoon, and that I had come away to tell her myself . . . . .

having another small matter to communicate at the same time."

"I am going straight home now," said Carlo, "and I shall tell her how pleased I am that all is settled as it is."

"And I say, Carlo, you will be in town to-morrow, I suppose, and we must see what is to be done about this ten thousand dollars, eh?" said the farmer.

"Yes, I will come in. I should very much like to have your advice upon the subject."

Regina had edged towards the door of the room while the foregoing words had been spoken, and was now close to Carlo as he stood with his hand on the door. She peeped out to the landing-place as he opened it, and seeing that there was nobody there or on the stairs, she stepped out after him, probably with the inten-tion of fulfilling her threat of making him begin all over again. But if so, he did not consent to begin from exactly the same starting-post. The farmer's lecture on love tactics had evidently not fallen on stony ground.

And then Signora Morini came into the *Salot-*

tino to superintend Aurora in the preparation of
the supper-table; and presently the lawyer and
his son, and Lao, the pale-faced clerk, came up
to their evening meal.

For a few minutes the farmer made no allu-
sion to the momentous news he had to tell; and
Regina sat on thorns, with her eyes fixed on her
plate, expecting the divulgation of her secret,
which she well knew her father would not spare
her.

At last it came. The farmer put his hand to
the flask of wine which stood on the table, and
first pouring a little into his own glass, filled the
glass of Meo, who sat next to him, according to
the approved fashion of Tuscan courtesy.

"Meo, my boy," said he, "let bygones be
bygones between you and me. Our friend,
Carlo, is well out of the mess and all right now.
And another time you won't be so much in a
hurry to think evil of an honest man."

"Yes, that is just it," put in the lawyer;
" so much in a hurry. Young men will be in a
hurry! But there, you can't put old heads on
young shoulders, can you, farmer?"

" No, I suppose not," said the farmer. "Things might have been different," continued he ; " at one time I hoped they might have gone all differently. But that is bygones now, like the rest. Things have taken a different turn, and perhaps it's all for the best; things generally *do* turn out for the best in this world, *I* believe. Any way, I've generally found it so, thanks be to the saints, as is right and proper."

" *Dice bene!* Signor Giovanni, *dice bene!* " said the Signora Maria, in a high cracked voice, with the eager approval with which Italian women are apt to hail and gather up any rare expressions of religious feeling which may fall from their lords and masters, or friends of the stronger and less pious sex.

" And so," continued the farmer, " I have no doubt that it is all for the best that Signor Carlo and my girl here have persuaded me to give my consent to their making a match of it."

The announcement, as it may be supposed, did not take any member of the company altogether by surprise. Yet it sent a little thrill like a slight electric shock through the little party to

hear that the interesting matter was definitely
settled. Regina kept her eyes steadfastly fixed
on her plate, and only showed by her rising colour
that she had heard her father's words. Meo
looked hard at her, being led instinctively to do
so by the unrecognised consciousness that it
must be just that which she would most wish at
the moment to avoid. The pale-faced clerk
looked at her surreptitiously. And the lawyer
and his wife exchanged glances with each other.

"I am sure I hope with all my heart," said
the lawyer, "that it may be for the happiness of all parties. Ten thousand crowns, it is
true . . . ."

"As for that part of the matter," interrupted
the farmer, "we don't know how that may turn
out. Maybe the lad will get the money, maybe
he won't. I am not one to count my chickens
before they are hatched!"

"Of course it stands to reason," said the
lawyer, "that if the money should not be
recovered, things can't be expected to stand as
they may if the anticipation of the recovery of
it is realised. For . . . ."

" Never let's mind about that," said the farmer, interrupting his old friend a second time. " We shall see how it turns out. Meantime I have given my consent to the match. And, if the Signora Maria will permit me, I will propose a health to the young people."

Of course the toast was enthusiastically accepted and drunk. And Regina sat shrinking and blushing on her chair, in a state of great discomfort.

" I think," said the farmer, when due honour had been done to his toast,—" I think that there is enough in the flask for the present company to drink another health ! "

" Sure there's plenty more in the cellar if there is not enough in the flask ! " said the Signora Maria ; " what's the other toast to be, Signor Giovanni ? "

" Well, it is to an old friend of all here, of whom I have a bit of news to tell you ;—to the widow Monaldi ! "

" The widow Monaldi ! " exclaimed two or three voices ;—" what, you don't mean that she is going to be married ? "

"You've hit it as pat as cheese on the maccaroni," replied the farmer ; "I am able to tell
you for certain that the widow is going to be
married !"

"Why, who did you hear it from ?" asked
Meo. "You did not know it, did you, when
we were speaking at dinner time."

"No ! I did not know it then. But it was
the widow herself who told me !" said the
farmer ; "I drove over there," he added, "a
little before supper."

"You were not long about it then, farmer,
for I saw you leave the house. I happened to
be at the studio window !" said the lawyer.

"No, I was not long about it !" said the
farmer with a chuckle. "I was not gone—
journey, visit, and all—over two hours."

"Well, but before we drink the health,
farmer," said the Signora Maria, "we must
know who the fortunate man is ! You have
not told us yet, who it is to be !"

"Ah ! who is it to be !" said the farmer with
a glance of his eye round the table ; "there has
been a many of the young fellows looking after

the widow by what I hear ;—and well they might, for she is a very beautiful woman, let alone a business turning in fifteen hundred dollars a year, and a pretty penny of savings ! "

" Yes ! " said the lawyer, " it'll be fifteen hundred a year, if it's worth a penny. I should say nearer two thousand. I know pretty well what the widow's business is ! "

" Well, Signor Giovanni, and who is the lucky man ? " said Meo, while all were eagerly waiting for the news, which they saw the farmer was minded to tantalise them a little with waiting for ; " who is it ? Whoever it is, he will make a dozen or so of fellows awfully savage and jealous," added Meo.

" No ! will he though, do you think ? " said the farmer, rolling his wide-opened eyes, with a queer expression of fun in them, round the circle. " Well ! that's natural too ! Men don't like to be cut out ! And particularly they don't like it, maybe, when they have been a trying it ever so long and ever so hard, and then they are cut out by somebody who didn't try at all till he went and *did* it. I dare say men don't like that, specially young fellows, who, as Signor Giacomo says, are always so much in a hurry, ha! ha! ha!"

"Well, come, farmer, tell us your news! don't make us wait for it any longer, there is a good man!" said the Signora Maria; "we have all got our glasses filled; but you haven't filled your own glass. Come, pour out a bumper, and out with the name!"

"No! thanks all the same, Signora Maria; I won't fill my own glass. Because, you know, folks don't drink their own health. I mean to marry the widow Monaldi!"

A start and a chorus of exclamations of surprise went round the table. The pale-faced clerk was betrayed by the excess of his astonishment into exclaiming *Per Bacco!* in an audible though suppressed voice; and was instantly looked down into the depths of confusion by a glance from the Signora Maria.

"And why not!" said she, being the first to recover from the shock which had been administered to the party. "Why not! I think it a very wise and a very good thing; and I wish

you joy with all my heart, Signore Giovanni.
The Signora Marta is a right good woman as
ever was, and was a real good wife to her first
husband."

"Thanks, Signora Maria! You and the
widow were always great friends, I know."

"But, Signor Giovanni, didn't you say that it
was the widow herself who told you the name
of the man she was going to marry?" asked
Meo.

"To be sure she did, Signor Meo! She told
me she was going to marry me!" said the
farmer with a twinkle in his eye.

"I suppose you told her first that you were
going to marry her?" said the lawyer, laughing.

"Well, we settled it between us one way or
another," said the farmer, "and we did not take
very long about it."

"On my conscience, you did not!" said the
lawyer, "if you mean to say that it was all done
since I saw you leave the house this afternoon."

"Yes! Signor Giacomo; it was all done and
settled since then. I had never spoken to the
widow about such a thing before. I hope the

young fellows you spoke of, Signor Meo, who are always in such a hurry, won't be *very* angry with me ! " said the farmer, enjoying his triumph exceedingly.

" Do you mean to continue the business ? " asked the lawyer.

" Oh, yes, we shall carry on the business ! It is too good to throw away by a great deal ! Our notion is that the young folks shall live at Sponda Lunga, and that Carlo shall continue to manage the business."

" Bravo, Signor Giovanni ! Nobody can say you don't know how to manage your own affairs !" said the lawyer. " Well, I think that whether the young fellows like it or not, you and the widow have both done very wisely. And I wish you joy with all my heart ! "

" Here's wishing you all happiness, and health to enjoy it, Signor Giovanni ! " said Meo ;—which did not at all interfere with his remarking to Lao, the pale-faced clerk, when they descended to the studio after supper, " Wasn't the old fellow proud of his conquest ! Much good may it do him, an old fool !—a double-distilled old idiot! A pretty life he'll have of it with that woman! Did you ever notice her eyes?"

Lao thought he rather *had* noticed her eyes; the loveliest eyes *he* had ever seen in a human head! as he professed with a smack of his lips.

"They are dangerous eyes, *Lao mio*,—devilish dangerous eyes! Take my word for it they bode no quiet life for that old ass of a farmer. Ask him what he thinks about those eyes a year hence!"

"Perhaps it might be better worth while talking to Signora Marta herself on the subject;" answered Lao with the air of a Don Giovanni.

"Ah! there'll be plenty ready to talk to her about that, and a little more beside," said Meo with a sneer; "not but what that consummate old ass would be likely to turn out a devil of a rough customer to deal with, mind you! They don't understand taking such things easy in the country, and are apt to cut up rough."

Nor did the Signora Maria's cordial expression of her anticipations of unbroken felicity to be derived to the farmer and his bride from their

happy union, prevent her saying to her husband
when they were alone together that night :

" As for him, one understands it well enough!
He's done well enough for himself! But whatever Marta Monaldi could have been thinking of
when she took him, I can't think for the life of
me! And she might have had . . . .!"

"Thinking of! why thinking of Ripalta to be
sure! And a very comfortable thought too!
Let the widow alone for knowing which side
her bread is buttered on!" returned the lawyer.

" Well! I wish she mayn't repent it before
the year's out, that's all! If ever there was
a tiger in his own house. . . . .!"

The contemplation of that noble beast esta-
blished " *dans ses meubles*" affected the Signora
Maria's imagination to such a degree that she
could only complete her sentence by a prolonged " ah-h-h !"

" Bah! bah! bah! the farmer likes to be
master at home ; and small blame to him!
She'll get on well enough with him, if she knows
how to take him. I don't see how she could
have done better! Think of that fellow, young

Simonetti! Suppose she had married him, where would she have been!" said the lawyer; "it makes one's flesh creep to think of Meo being hand and glove, as one may say, with that fellow!"

"Ah-h-h! more's the pity. If it had not been for him Meo would never have gone and offended the farmer in that way, and things might ha' been very different! Ah-h-h!" said the good mother and wife, mixing just a sufficient flavour of reproach in the tone of her ejaculation, as good wives will occasionally, to intimate her feeling that more might be said on the subject of the lawyer having permitted her son to form such an intimacy, if she were inclined to be severely just.

Meanwhile Carlo had returned to Sponda Lunga, and had told his own story to the widow. He could not help feeling that it came a good deal easier, or at least pleasanter in the telling, by reason of the story which the widow also had to tell him. It was impossible for him to have remained blind to the fact that the gentle and kindly widow would have fain promoted

him from manager to master of herself and her
thriving business. And the idea of the pain
that he should be giving to one, to whom he
owed so much of kindness and consideration of
every kind, in telling that any such consum-
mation was wholly out of the question, had been
very disagreeable to him. Now the farmer's
veni-vidi-vici had put an end to all that. They
could exchange congratulations; and no one
would be left out of the happiness of the time.

"*Alfine*, Signore Carlo!" cried the widow,
meeting him at the door with a gentle smile;
"you have been so long bringing me your news,
that somebody else has brought it before you!
It has made me very happy, *ve'*! For though I
knew it would all come right sooner or later, I
fretted over the thing more than enough! But
it's all well that ends well, isn't it?"

"And you have heard all about how it was
found out, and of that unfortunate poor good-
for-nothing Simonetti?"

"Oh, it is too shocking!" said the widow,
shaking her head sadly. But she smiled again,
though she drooped the eyelids over her eyes a

little as she spoke, when she added : " But that
is not the only news I have heard, Signor
Carlo ! "

" What, about me too ! What can it be ! "
said Carlo with a roguish laugh in his eye.

" Well, have you not something else to tell
me ? " said the widow, still dropping her eyes to
the ground, but with a dimpling smile about
the mouth, that was almost creaming over into
a laugh.

" Well, perhaps there might have been something else to tell if you had not heard it already,
Signora Marta ! But is all the telling to be on
my side ? Have you nothing to tell me, eh,
Signora Marta ? "

" Well, perhaps I might have had something
else to tell if you had not heard it already,
Signore Carlo ! " said the widow, echoing his
words.

" In short, we both know all about the other's
doings, and know that we have both been
amusing ourselves in the same way ! Is that
about it, Signora Marta ? Eh ? " said Carlo.

" Well, I should think not ! At least I am

sure that I have not been asking anybody to marry me!" said the widow.

"Well, you won't deny that you have said 'yes,' when somebody else asked you?" rejoined Carlo.

"Indeed, but I do deny any such thing. I never said 'yes,' to anybody at all!" insisted the widow.

"Well! come; you did not say 'no!' And I am very glad you did not, Signora Marta," said Carlo speaking more seriously; "for Signor Giovanni is a right good fellow, and I think you will be as happy as I wish you; and that is saying a good deal."

"Thank you, Signor Carlo! I am sure that would content me in the way of happiness! And you won't doubt that I wish you everything you can wish yourself with equal sincerity. Come, let us go to supper! By the bye, I forgot all this time to tell you that there is another printed letter for you, just like the one you had last time. It came about an hour before you returned home."

"It is an invitation to wait on the Com-

missary again to-morrow !   To think of me, who
never knew what a Commissary of Police looked
like till the other day, having come to live
among them in this way!" said Carlo, looking
at the printed form, with its lacunes filled up
with scrawling writing.

"What can it be about this time?" asked
the widow.

"Well! I hope that it is something about
the discovery of the ten thousand dollars ! We
shall see to-morrow ! "

And so the widow and Carlo sate down to
one of the few more tête-à-tête suppers they
were to eat together. And it will be readily
conceived that the meal was not a dull one from
want of matter for conversation.

CHAPTER IX.

CARLO RECOVERS HIS INHERITANCE.

THE next day at twelve o'clock, the hour named in the "invitation," Carlo found himself once again at the sordid-looking door of the dirty police bureau; and this time, without any inquiring or looking about him, went straightway up the steep narrow staircase. Upon this occasion, however, he was not allowed to walk into the crowded ante-room, and wait unnoticed till he was wanted. At the top of the stair he found a red-collared official, evidently on the look-out for him, who, saluting him with much show of respect, requested him to walk into the private room of the Signor Commissario; and following his guide by another route than that which he followed on the previous occasion, he was thus brought into a somewhat more com-

fortable room than that in which the discom-
fiture of Andrea Simonetti had taken place;
and there was somewhat startled at finding,
besides the Commissary who had conducted the
examination the other day, the Commissary of
Pescia, and . . . . the Reverend Pasquale
Mommi !

Both rose as he entered, and made him, the
first a smirking, the second a sulky bow, and re-
seated themselves.

"I told you the other day, Signor Caroli, that
I thought it likely I might find it necessary to
trouble you to call on me again ; and doubtless
you can guess what the matter in hand is."

Carlo bowed and remained silent.

"I have thought that it would be pleasanter to
all parties," pursued the Commissary, "specially
to his Reverence, and also more consistent with
the respect which we all have for the Holy Church,
to talk over the little matter we have to settle
privately. I do not see the necessity—as far
that is, as matters have hitherto gone—to let
this affair be a cause of scandal—a result, you
know, Signor *Parroco*, which ought always to

be avoided as far as possible. Do you not agree
with me, your Reverence, that it would be better
to arrange this little affair among ourselves here
in this room, if we can ?"

The priest gave a grunt and a dogged sort of
nod of his head, which the Commissary accepted
as an assent.

"I need not, perhaps," he resumed, "go over
all the history of the case very minutely. Signor
Caroli's mother won a very large prize in the
lottery—some ten thousand dollars—which were
paid to her in gold by the administration at
Florence. It can be proved that she had this
money in her house at Uzzano on the evening
before her lamented and very sudden death.
The money could not be found after her death;
but just that sum was found in a very singular
hiding place in the house of this reverend gentleman at Uzzano. The reverend gentleman declared his ignorance of the existence there of any
such sum ; and suggested that it had probably
been placed there by some one of his predecessors, to whom it might have been entrusted for
pious uses."

"I was not bound to give any account of the sum in any way," growled the priest.

"Certainly not! Quite right, your Reverence! And you, feeling indignant at the search of your premises, exercised your right of refusing all information to the officers, and went so far as to suggest other sources from whence the money might have come. And then, when it is found that the people of the administration of the lottery are able to recognise the paper of the rouleaux in which the money was rolled, and thus it becomes certain that the money found in your house is the same with that paid by the lottery to the Signora Barbara Caroli, your Reverence declares that the money was consigned to you for pious uses by that lady. Now it is true that you were not bound to give us any information upon the subject. But, at the same time, it cannot be denied, Signor *Parroco*, that the magistrates are apt to conceive a prejudice against people whose statements thus vary."

"I can't help that, Signor *Commissario*," growled the priest.

"Certainly not, Signor *Parroco!*" returned

the Commissary, with unabated suavity; "but nevertheless it may be worth while looking at the matter a little as it will present itself to them. If the Signora Barbara Caroli made over to you the very large sum of money in question for pious uses and for her soul's welfare, she must have done so during the last few hours of her life."

"Well, Signor *Commissario,* and at what period of life, pray, are such considerations most in the habit of forcing themselves on the consciences of sinners? What is it that we usually see in such cases?" said the priest.

"Very well put, Signor *Parroco,* and very true! Only we must remember that the magistrates will be likely to ask themselves whether it is usual to find dying penitents carrying forth their money in the dead of the night to consign it into the hands of their spiritual advisers in the churchyard?" said the Commissary, with a hard and shrewd look into the priest's face.

Inured from their earliest seminary years upwards to conceal their thoughts and feelings, and to forbid their features from telling tales

respecting them, the priesthood of Rome have
generally a remarkable power of face, and the
Commissary got little by his hard look at the
gross features of the Reverend Pasquale Mommi.
Nevertheless, he had not been able to suppress
altogether a little start when mention of the
churchyard was made.

"I don't know what you mean," he said.
"Who ever spoke of the woman coming into the
churchyard? I'll wager it was many a year she
had not come into the churchyard before she
was brought there to be buried, *povera santa
anima!* Our people at Uzzano, Signor *Commissario*, are not fond of coming into the churchyard."

"But, Signor *Prete*, the dying woman was
found on the steps which lead from the town-
street to the churchyard. How do you account
for her being found there?"

"Once more, Signor *Commissario*, I am not
bound to account for any circumstance of the
sort. But anybody may see for themselves that
nothing is more natural than that the widow
should have been on those steps on her way back

from a visit to my house to her own house. She would pass from my door along the piazza in front of the church, and so down the steps at the west front."

" Then you admit, Signor *Parroco*, that the widow Caroli paid you a visit at the *Cura* on the evening before her death?" asked the *Commissario*.

" No ; I don't. I neither deny nor admit anything," said the priest, doggedly.

" Quite right! Signor *Parroco !* quite right. But I should be deceiving you, if I left you in ignorance of the fact that we have other reasons for thinking that the visit paid to you in the course of that night by the widow Caroli was paid not in the house of the *Cura* but in the churchyard !"

" I don't know what you mean, Signor *Commissario*, and I must say that I think it hardly consistent with your duty to make insinuations of such a nature, without having the means of substantiating them. That I saw the Signora Barbara Caroli in the churchyard ! It is perfectly preposterous ! And I cannot conceive what can have put such an absurdity into your head !" said the priest, with a very well performed show of virtuous indignation.

"Every word you say is quite true, *reverendo mio signore*," answered the Commissary, with imperturbable good humour. " It is true; and I perfectly agree with you that I should be gravely overstepping the limits of my duty were I to hazard insinuations such as I have pointed to, without having due and sufficient means for the substantiation of them. And I feel convinced that if your Reverence will give your attention to the matter in a judicious and conciliatory spirit, we shall agree equally well to the end. Our object, you know, the object of all of us here, is to arrange this affair satisfactorily without giving occasion for scandal."

" I think you have given occasion enough for scandal as it is, searching the house of a parish priest with the assistance of *giandarmi* in the open day !" snorted the priest.

" Not at all, Signor *Parroco !* No scandal at all ! May it not happen to anybody that the police may have reason to suspect that there is something they are bound to look after in such or such a house, without any sort of blame to the proprietor. *Che diamine!* Suppose we had been told that Italian translations of Protestant Bibles had been introduced into your house without your knowledge? No! no! there need be no scandal at all. If, as I hope, we are able to arrange this affair amicably among ourselves in this room, there will be no sort of scandal. We shall say that it is all right—that the search was all a mistake—and it will be all right. Should we fail to settle the matter amicably before we bring this sitting to a conclusion, then indeed it is to be feared that very painful scandal, and results even more disagreeable still, may follow. But I am convinced that your good sense will see the matter in the same light that we do, when you have the same means of forming an opinion. And I wish to be quite frank with you. You shall have all the means that we have for forming an opinion on the subject."

" Signor Pecchi," continued the *Commissario*, addressing his colleague from Pescia, " will you have the goodness to bring that little girl here whom I left in the care of my wife? Now you will see, *reverendo signore*, whether I threw out insinuations recklessly."

Signor Pecchi left the room, and returned in a few minutes with little Beppina Trilli. The child appeared terribly frightened at first, and was by no means tranquillised by finding her parish priest among the formidable assembly she was called on to face. She recognised Carlo Caroli, however, with a shy look; and when the Commissary asked her whether she did not know those gentlemen, she edged up to him, and stole her little brown hand into his.

" You know this reverend gentleman also, do you not, *bambina mia?*" said the Commissary.

" Yes, sir!" answered Beppina, but without moving from Carlo's knee.

" I think the best way will be for you to ask her the few questions we want her to answer, Signor Caroli. She is very shy, poor little thing; and she knows you," said the Commissary.

" Do you remember the talk we had, *Beppina mia*, one day under the great trees behind the castle at Uzzano ? " asked Carlo, gently putting his arm round the frightened little creature, as she stood at his knee.

" *Si, Signor Carlo ! mi rammento benone !* " said the child, looking up with her great blue eyes into his face.

" And do you remember the day your poor mother died, *buona anima ?* "

The child answered only by a nod ; and the silent tears came into her eyes.

" And now tell me, Beppina, what you told me then about your being sent to fetch the *parroco* to your mother ? "

And then he drew from her the whole account of her experiences of that terrible night, given without the smallest variation from her former statement. No assurances of the non-existence of any bogy in that time and place had sufficed to convince her, or to induce her to move from her earnest statement that she *had* seen a bogy attired as she described, and acting as she had asserted.

The Commissary keenly watched the face of the priest the while. It was abundantly evident that the reverend gentleman felt himself less and less at ease, as the narrative of the child proceeded. And when the awful fact of the bogy having had black legs was distinctly testified to, he almost broke down. He quite sufficiently understood from what the Commissary had said, and from the general tone he had taken, that it was intended to allow the matter to be hushed up, if he would consent to surrender the money quietly. But it went very, very much against the grain with him to do so. And he had come to Lucca at the invitation of the Commissary fully determined to brazen the matter out, and stick to the fact, that it was impossible to prove that the widow Caroli, moved by her conscience and the desire of benefiting her own soul and that of her husband, had not made over the money to him willingly and intentionally. He thought that in a case of the kind, a sense of the necessity of defending one of the most valuable sources of Church emolument would assure to him the support of his bishop, and of the Church generally; and that thus backed he could defy the legal authorities to take the money from him. There was the legate, too, at Florence, in case of need; and a court which had been of late years becoming more and more anxious not to offend that of the Holy See. And probably, had his own previous character been other than it was, and had there been no circumstances of a nature to cast a scandalous, and perhaps even still worse, a ridiculous light on the matter, he would have judged rightly.

But now things began to assume a different aspect. Here were people ready to complain because he was not to be found when sent for to administer the last sacraments to a dying woman. Here was the story of the child, the true explanation of which had evidently at once suggested itself to these Commissaries. He began to think that he could not venture to play a game, which, if it went against him, would bring absolute ruin and disgrace upon him. And the "hushing up" method of concluding the matter, even at the cost of abandoning all the golden dreams in which he had been revelling, began to assume an acceptable appearance in his eyes.

To " hush up " a crime is, according to Anglo-Saxon notions, little creditable in any honest man, and is absolutely criminal in those whose special duty it is to bring wrong-doing to light. But in Italy all these matters are judged very differently. The teaching of the Roman Catholic Church is at the bottom of this state of public opinion. *Scandal* is in the eyes of the Church often as great, sometimes a greater evil than the original fault itself. And it is always well to avoid it. It is always good to " hush up," if some measure of substantial justice can be combined with such a course. In the eyes of the lay magistracy, in such a case as that in question, the prime object would be that the man should have the money, who ought to have it. That result being attained, it would seem that nothing further could be desired, or be in any way necessary. That due punishment should light upon the wrong-doer, and that this should be cared for on public grounds of social security and morality,—this would not in any wise occur to the Italian forensic mind. The quality of moral indignation is scarcely to be traced as existent in the country.

If, therefore, it could be contrived that this important sum of money could be restored to the rightful owner without " scandal," and without causing further trouble or inconvenience to anybody, such a result would appear eminently desirable to all the persons engaged in the inquiry.

It began to seem likely that this end might be attained. The Reverend Pasquale Mommi, with a consciousness of former occasions of collision with the superior ecclesiastical authorities, began to perceive that the story, as it stood, was not one which it would do to go into any court, civil or ecclesiastical, with.

" We clergy have very hard times of it! " he said, with an attempt at an appearance of good-humoured *bonhomie ;* " if the child could not make me hear, when she rang the night bell at the *Cura*, it was because I had been knocked up and was sleeping soundly. As to her story of what she saw, it is too absurd for serious con-

sideration. The poor child was in an excited
state of mind, and was frightened by the wind
among the trees, and the shadows. But I know
how hardly a priest is sure to be judged. I
know how much would be made of these chance
circumstances. I know how bitterly the gifts of
the faithful are grudged to the ministers of the
altar. And God knows that I never was greedy
after money. My life is simple enough, and will
bear looking into in every part, I venture to
assert. And if Signor Carlo Caroli has so great
a desire to possess this money, in heaven's name
let him take it! If he has no scruple of
conscience in thus frustrating the intention of
his departed mother in favour of her own soul,
and his father's,—I say let him take the
dollars;—and much good may they do him!
It has generally been found that the spoils of
the Church have not much profited the spoiler.
And I am one of those who believe in God's
government of the world, and hold that what
has been shall be! But I say nothing!
Perhaps Signor Caroli might think it decent,
under the circumstances, to bestow the charity

of a few masses on his parents so lately departed this life;—one of them without having had the sacraments!"

"Supposing me to be in possession of ten thousand crowns, Signor *Parroco*," replied Carlo, gravely; "I should not object to expend two hundred of them in the manner you speak of."

"Supposing you were in possession! Why you are in possession of them! *I* have not got the money! These gentlemen have taken it forcibly from me, and have doubtless given it to you!"

"Not so, Signor *Parroco!* We have no authority to do anything of the kind. I am delighted to perceive that this little misunderstanding is likely to be brought to an amicable termination. But it cannot be done quite in the manner you speak of. See, the dollars are here," continued the Commissary, opening an iron safe in the wall of his room;—"all safe in their original rouleaux. All that is needed is that you should give us a receipt in full for them, stating that they were taken by us from

your house, and have been in our custody ever
since, and that you now yourself hand them
over to Signor Carlo Caroli as a part of the
inheritance of his mother, happening to be in
your hands."

"And suppose that, having the money in my
possession, seeing that you admit you have not
the right to dispose of it, I should decline to
hand over to Signor Caroli money entrusted
to me for a different purpose?" said the
priest.

"In that case we should be obliged, with
great sorrow, to own that all our attempts at an
amicable arrangement were at an end; the
money would for the present remain where it is;
and we should be forced to make the matter
the subject of a regular process in the civil
and in the ecclesiastical courts," said the
Commissary.

"Yes! I know! I know all about it! I
know what chance of justice a poor parish priest
would have! As I said, we priests have a hard
time of it in this world. I am too wise to feel
any inclination to go to law. It is not a seemly

position for a minister of the gospel! What is it you want me to sign?" said the priest.

The Commissary drew up a receipt in due form, which the Reverend Pasquale Mommi duly signed, discharging Signore Pecchi, Commissary for the city and district of Pescia, from all responsibility in the matter of the ten thousand dollars removed by the latter from the *Cura* of Uzzano. Then Carlo signed a similar receipt, vouching the payment of the same sum to him by the Reverend Pasquale Mommi. And when this was fairly done, the priest got himself out of the room, with such form of salutation as he could bring himself to utter; the dollars were consigned to Carlo; and the three men left in the room looked at each other in silence for a minute or two, after the first was gone.

"What a sly old scoundrel it is!" said the Commissary, smiling; "I congratulate you, Signor Caroli, on the recovery of your inheritance! I think you would have got it all the same, if the old rogue had pushed us before the tribunal, as he might have done. But it is much better,—very far better, as it is."

In which sentiment Carlo cordially agreed, and proceeded to get himself and his money to the lawyer's house as best and quickest he might. He could not bear to carry the money to his home without first telling the news of his success to Regina and her father. Besides, he had come to agree with Signor Simonetti in thinking that the widow's house might not be quite a safe place for a large sum of money; and he thought that he could not do better than consult Lawyer Morini on the disposal of it.

CHAPTER X.

Our story is even as a tale that is told! in a literal sense certainly. But on the banks of the Serchio, it is not yet quite so in the metaphorical sense of the phrase. For there are still children and grandchildren of Carlo Caroli and his wife Regina on the Ripalta farm there, among whom the strange and true story of the Dream Numbers is still remembered, and brought forth at times on winter nights from the stores of the family archives for the admiration, wonder, and sympathy of listening guests.

They are no longer farmers on the lands, for old Giovanni Bartoli did not go to the long holiday beneath the sod of the pretty little churchyard under the shade of the Pisan mountain till, by help of the great lottery prize, and the widow Monaldi's savings, joined to his own, he had accomplished the great ambition of his life, and become the owner of the estate. Improvements, general progress, and the movement of population resulting from recent political changes, have made the lands much more valuable than they were at the time of the last great inundation of the dangerous Serchio. And it may be hoped that more scientific improvement in the dykes and other means of security have very much diminished the chances of a recurrence of the great calamity.

The farmer thus died a considerable landed proprietor. And it was thus rendered very proper that the descendants of Carlo Caroli and Regina his wife should take the name of Bartoli-Caroli; and so they are known at the present day, and will be, it may be hoped, for many a generation to come.

The widow Monaldi remained childless in her second marriage, as she had been in her first. But her marriage with the farmer was none the less felt by both the parties mainly concerned, and acknowledged by that great public opinion which considers itself the special judge of such matter, to have been a great success. If little treble voices and the sunshine which children make be wanted as an ingredient in a perfectly happy home, they were rarely wanting in the new house at Ripalta. And the gentle Signora Marta used—and as Regina was wont to declare, somewhat abused—the grand-maternal privilege of enjoying all the pleasure of spoiling children, without incurring any of the responsibility and trouble connected with the needful counteracting processes. It was very pleasant to the kindly and indulgent—widow I had nearly written, by the force of the habit of three volumes on my hand—Signora Bartoli I should say—it was very agreeable to her to cram little mouths with *buccellati*, thickly spread with jam, and leave the subsequent dosings with purgative waters from Monte Catini to mamma.

Caroli continued to carry on the wheelwright business very successfully under the new firm of

Bartoli and Caroli, till on the death of the old farmer, at an advanced age, he disposed of the business advantageously. He continued, however, to possess, and his children, in obedience to his wishes, still continue to possess, the old house at Uzzano, with the bit of vineyard and chestnut wood attached to it. Very little has been done to it;—merely enough to keep it from going altogether to ruin. But it served for the purpose of a pleasant *villegiatura* during the great heats of July and August, and Caroli and his wife and young brood were often made happy by a holiday excursion thither at those times. More than one successor has followed the Reverend Pasquale Mommi in the position he held, without following him in the path he trod, since the day of the Dream Numbers and the results of them. But as long as he remained in the *Cura* the Reverend Pasquale Mommi never failed to wait on Signor Caroli, on the occasion of every visit he made to his old mountain home, doing no more than his duty in the paying of such attentions, as he always declared, towards a benefactor to the Church and one of his most distinguished parishioners.

There may seem to remain one word more to be said respecting the subsequent fortunes of one or two other of those in whom the reader has been kind enough to interest himself. But the doing so brings us to the opening of another rather remarkable series of events which cannot be related here. One of the results of the crime of Andrea Simonetti and its more immediate consequences, was to cause all the long-hoarded wealth of the old usurer to become the inheritance of that sister who had shown her housewifely qualities so inopportunely on the occasion of the ownership of the handkerchief stolen from her brother. And one of the results of this appropriation of old Simonetti's hoardings was that our friend, Meo Morini, sought and obtained that lady's hand in marriage. And the ultimate consequences of this marriage produced certain complications and relationship between Meo and his convict brother-in-law, which abundantly punished the former for the sin of being induced by such motives to make such a mar-

riage, and led to a train of circumstances which
may possibly form the subject of another
Lucchese domestic chronicle.

THE END.

BRADBURY, EVANS, AND CO., PRINTERS, WHITEFRIARS.

www.ingramcontent.com/pod-product-compliance
Lightning Source LLC
Chambersburg PA
CBHW020938030726

47496CB00005B/1249